Other Places

Conversation Pieces

A Small Paperback Series from Aqueduct Press
Subscriptions available: www.aqueductpress.com

About the Aqueduct Press
Conversation Pieces Series

The feminist engaged with sf is passionately interested in challenging the way things are, passionately determined to understand how everything works. It is my constant sense of our feminist-sf present as a grand conversation that enables me to trace its existence into the past and from there see its trajectory extending into our future. A genealogy for feminist sf would not constitute a chart depicting direct lineages but would offer us an ever-shifting, fluid mosaic, the individual tiles of which we will probably only ever partially access. What could be more in the spirit of feminist sf than to conceptualize a genealogy that explicitly manifests our own communities across not only space but also time?

Aqueduct's small paperback series, Conversation Pieces, aims to both document and facilitate the "grand conversation." The Conversation Pieces series presents a wide variety of texts, including short fiction (which may not always be sf and may not necessarily even be feminist), essays, speeches, manifestoes, poetry, interviews, correspondence, and group discussions. Many of the texts are reprinted material, but some are new. The grand conversation reaches at least as far back as Mary Shelley and extends, in our speculations and visions, into the continually-created future. In Jonathan Goldberg's words, "To look forward to the history that will be, one must look at and retell the history that has been told." And that is what Conversation Pieces is all about.

L. Timmel Duchamp

Jonathan Goldberg, "The History That Will Be" in Louise Fradenburg and Carla Freccero, eds., *Premodern Sexualities* (New York and London: Routledge, 1996)

Published by Aqueduct Press
PO Box 95787
Seattle, WA 98145-2787
www.aqueductpress.com

10 9 8 7 6 5 4 3 2 1
ISBN: 978-1-61976-115-5

Original Block Print of Mary Shelley by Justin Kempton:
www.writersmugs.com

Acknowledgments

The previously published stories contain minor revisions: "The Rising Up," published in *See the Elephant Magazine*; "Twelve Sisters, Twelve Sisters, Ten," published in *Black Apples*; "How to Be a Foreigner" and "The Alien Came over the Hill," published in *Daily Science Fiction*.

Printed in the USA by Applied Digital Imaging

Conversation Pieces
Volume 51

Other Places

by
Karen Heuler

Contents

The Rising Up

Franzy was suddenly back in school and completely unprepared for the history test.

But that wasn't why everyone was staring at her and smiling. No, *smirking*. A few had turned their heads and whispered something behind their hands to their neighbors as she entered the classroom. A woman off to the side pointed at her.

Franzy stopped and looked down at herself. It was horrible! She was only wearing a bra—a cheap, tired, gray-looking bra. She should have thrown it out years ago. But the woman had pointed at her crotch. When Franzy shifted her eyes she saw a penis sticking out— erect and out of place. She could feel the annoying jitteriness of it. She was naked and she had a penis. Taking a test was out of the question. She should never have come here.

She turned and ran. Laughter followed her.

Franzy passed a coat closet near the outside doors and found a tee shirt, pants, socks, shoes—everything she needed. She tucked the penis, which kept twitching, into the pants. It was a silly mistake, bringing it with her! She should have left it home.

It was much colder outside than she'd realized. She should have grabbed a coat. Franzy turned to go back into the school, but all the doors were locked, and it looked deserted and decaying. She hadn't visited it in decades.

It began to snow. Her shoes were little ballet slippers, the kind she'd worn when she was eight and dreamed of dancing. She turned the corner onto a highway, where big rigs zoomed past, blasting horns that made her jump from one pile of snow to another.

The snowdrifts themselves were starting to look like huddling, looming shapes. One of them collapsed, burying Franzy in a cold white tunnel. The whiteness made an artificial light. She could see people sitting on their haunches, huddled forward, their shoulders touching the top of the snowbank. She scuttled in next to them.

"You have to be quiet," the man to her right said. "We have to discuss this. We're all trapped in this dream, trying to figure it out."

"This is a dream?" Franzy asked.

The woman to her left looked at her pityingly. "Of course it's a dream. Haven't you even tried to wake up yet?"

"No, I haven't," Franzy whispered. "How do you know it's a dream?"

Without a word, the man took a gun out of his pocket and shot her in the heart.

Franzy gasped, held her hand over her chest, saw the blood, and cried out, "Why did you do that?"

"You should have woken up or died," he said. "That's what would normally happen. And you're not dead. You're not even bleeding."

Franzy looked down at her white shirt (had it always been a white shirt?) and saw there was no blood. There was a bullet hole, though. "I don't feel any pain," she said in wonder.

"It's a government takeover, or a corporate takeover. If you run straight ahead you'll see the armies. We're meeting here to find a strategy to fight them."

"What can we do?" Franzy whispered. It all made sense, except for the conspiracy part. Government or corporate? How come they didn't know?

"It was the Rising Up," the woman to her left said. "You don't remember, do you? After the death of everything we knew and loved, we rose up. We shouted no. And those on the very edges, left and right, closed in to silence us. We just don't know if it was the politicians or the greedy capitalists; they were hand in hand, anyway. They put us all to sleep. The waking world is ruled by them, now."

"Why can't we wake up?" Franzy cried. It seemed so urgent! She tried to tell herself it was time to open her eyes, but nothing happened.

"They've locked us in," the man to her right said. "We have to find a way to break through. We're meeting in hidden places everywhere, assembling our army. Are you with us?"

"I am," Franzy said. "I am."

"Then rise up!" he said. The woman on her other side jumped up at the same time and said, "Rise up!" and rows and rows of people Franzy hadn't seen rose up and burst through the snow banks, all of them looking very Soviet, with their fists in the air, shouting.

A line of trucks slowed down on the highway beside them, and people leaped out to join their fight. They lined up in phalanxes facing a dark line on the horizon, which zoomed at them in an unnatural way.

The enemy's advance guard contained helmeted people, mostly men, wearing thick gray suits. They had scarves tied over the lower half of their faces, so only their eyes showed, evil and sharp.

"Prepare your weapons!" the man to her right shouted, and everyone bent down and made snowballs.

"Snowballs?" Franzy cried, but even as she doubted it, she saw the snowballs lobbed at the enemy bursting into explosions. When she looked down, she saw piles of small bombs all around them. Her army was packing each small bomb into a snowball, so she did too.

The bombs felt light and soft, almost like beanbags. They seemed to grab the snow packed around them, forming a hard shell. *So that's what makes them burst,* she thought.

The enemy had their own weapons, sharp ice-arrows that went through people and came out pink. *That's blood,* she thought.

"Watch what you think," the man to her right said.

"It isn't blood," the woman to her left said. "It's paint."

Franzy's mind went swiftly from blood to paint, and she saw that the people who'd been stabbed were fine. The paint just made them stumble a little, perhaps adding weight. Indeed, up ahead, a man completely covered in paint fell down.

The advance guard began to run away as the army behind them came closer, no doubt afraid that they would be crushed under the wheels of their own forces.

Franzy froze with fear. The enemy soldiers were the size of buildings, coming at them like tanks, ships, buses, trucks, ready to ride over them.

They cast enormous shadows. Franzy looked down at the shadows and saw the edge of one come loose. She bent down, picked at it, and it pulled up one piece. It was connected to the advancing army.

"They're made of paper!" she cried. The enemy soldiers began to burst and burn from the bombs her side threw, and the snow made their lower edges curl up.

"They're paper!" the man to her right repeated, and she heard the word *paper* spread through the ranks.

"They thought they could fool us with images," the woman to her left said. The people murmured, relieved. But it turned out that their own tanks and cars and trucks were also paper.

The man to her right looked at her with disappointment. "That isn't right at all. Now we'll have to march."

As they all began to march over the monumental paper army, dirtying them underfoot, Franzy felt somewhat foolish. She had thought one thing and was frightened, but then it had all worked out

"Nothing has worked out," the man to her right said. "You've given in to the diversions in the dream, that's all. Try to remember who you are in real life. We will never wake if we get caught up in the dream."

Franzy looked at herself, in a uniform of navy blue jeans and a jeans jacket, just like all the others. Those clothes looked more like her; maybe she was making headway.

Her bladder felt full to bursting. That might wake her up, she thought, but it didn't. Franzy stepped over to a snowbank and pulled out her penis. It was a great relief to pee, and very convenient to have a penis. It was hard to put back in her pants, however, since it had grown a bit when she grabbed it, but she fought it back and then returned to battle.

It was spring and the snow had melted. The highway was deserted, the armies gone. Far off, the city glittered. Railroad tracks ran straight towards it, and a raised station perched off to the side. Franzy heard the blasts of the train coming, and she ran for the station as it pulled in for a brief stop, just managing to get on before the conductor yelled, "All aboard!"

Franzy panted as she stumbled into a seat. The man to her right was, as usual, to her right. For a moment, they looked out the window as the train slowly rocked forward. Fields stretched into the distance.

"Big Ag," he said. "That's what it is. It's not the government at all. They'd never be organized enough to pull it off. Big Ag can spray the crops with anything." As he spoke, a crop duster ran across the field, releasing a plume of something that crept in through the closed windows and made them all cough.

The woman to her left said, "It's why we've got to fight this together. There's a dream machine in the city. They've set it so we can never truly wake up. We have to wake up." She clutched Franzy's arm. "Even if we all die."

Franzy looked along the car and saw the whole compartment filled with people determined to fight and win. They all looked prepared to die.

"You can't think of dying," the man to her right said.

Franzy understood and stopped thinking about it. The train rushed onward, and the soldiers all started singing a World War II song, something sad but brave. Franzy wore a bias-cut dress, clinging and figure-enhancing, but her penis broke the line. It had to be adjusted. It was inconvenient, to say the least.

The man to her right raised his eyebrows at her and frowned, as the music over the public address system shifted from war to romance. He tapped the back of her hand. "We're fighting for connection, for the freedom to connect with each other." His eyes became moist and his voice husky.

As he leaned closer to her, Franzy could see over his shoulder that soldiers all down the rows were leaning into each other, embracing, their hands wandering, their voices sweet. *This is why all wars are fought*, she thought, *to find out who to love*. The man to her right ran his hand over both her organs, seeming not to prefer one to the other, and she rejoiced at the new pleasure her penis gave her.

The woman to her left cried, "This is not the reason we fight! They are controlling us!" Franzy wanted to follow her body's instincts without prejudice. How could something so insistent and natural be wrong? But the woman to her left stood up and shouted, "Tsunami!"

Every head looked out the window. They saw the bare ocean bed merely ten feet below them as the train sped round the cliff toward the city. Whales and porpoises and fishing boats struggled to find their purchase in the silt. Franzy raised her eyes from the dry seabed to a wave as tall as a skyscraper running towards them.

The soldiers began to scream.

"No!" the woman to her left cried. "Think of something else! It looks like clouds, doesn't it? Huge clouds, maybe a thunderstorm?"

And Franzy saw that, yes, it was clouds banked up on the horizon like a wave. The dry seabed was just a low tide, coming in swiftly now. The whale splashed, waiting for the water to rise some more, and the fisherman straightened his nets.

The whale will be safe, Franzy thought with relief. Meanwhile, the whole army was straightening itself out, nodding at the person they'd been touching just a moment earlier. Not exactly sheepish, just restored.

As they headed back inland, Franzy asked, "This dream machine—where is it? What does it look like? How does it work?"

"It's a sound," the man on her right said. "A lulling, hypnotic sound." And indeed Franzy could hear light beeps in the background. "The machine keeps us locked to impressions in our dreams, to sights and sounds and words that suggest other sights and sounds and words. We're trapped by our own imaginations."

"How do you know?" she asked.

"I put it there," he said, a sob breaking his voice.

The train car hushed, and soldiers leaned towards him, their heads turned slightly so they could hear better.

"I made it," he whispered. "They wanted machines to soothe the cattle at slaughter. I made a machine that kept them happy even with the hammer, the knife, the shock. And they used it."

"Big Ag," someone hissed.

He lifted his head. "The corporations, too, you understand. They made more money; the meat was tender and didn't cry. The public loves stories of that kind, where they do no harm and still get fat."

"*We* are the public," Franzy said. "So that's insulting." She glanced down at her loose sweatshirt and pants, at her pudgy hand. Her penis was hidden somewhere below the belly fat, she assumed. All the soldiers looked a little overfed as well, with beer bellies and puffy second chins.

She felt a little hungry. "I haven't eaten in days," she said.

"In days!" the army chanted behind her.

"Or had anything to drink!" the woman to her left cried. She wore leggings, a loose shirt, and crocs.

"Can you wear crocs to war?" Franzy asked, and a shiver ran down the train car. The soldiers got thinner, sitting up straight, checking their belts or their guns.

"We're almost there!" the man on her right called out. "Soldiers, prepare for a rapid assault on the rooftops!"

With that, the train turned into a freight elevator, packed with soldiers. Franzy stood wedged shoulder to shoulder with the man to her right and the woman to her left. They sped upwards so rapidly her ears popped. The whole car filled with popping sounds, and the soldiers laughed and shifted in amusement.

They spilled out of the freight elevator onto a huge roof, with the city's other roofs exposed all around them. It was twilight. Lights blinked on all around the city and in the sky. A tall blue tower rose above them. Franzy felt a hum in her ears.

"This is so beautiful," she said. "A shame to destroy it."

The army kept coming out of the elevators, more and more of them, crowding and pushing Franzy and her companions closer to the edge of the roof. "I don't like heights," she said nervously.

"You've forgotten why you're here," the man to her right said, and pushed her off the roof. "Remember not to think about hitting the earth."

At first, Franzy felt terrified, then she noticed people in windows watching her fall. She wondered what they were doing behind those windows, and her fall slowed until she could move in any direction she wanted. Flying. It wasn't fast or particularly high. She zeroed in on a woman staring out a window. The woman opened her window and said, "You can only fly in dreams, you know."

Ah, Franzy thought, *I'd almost forgotten I was in a dream.*

Franzy tried to fly up to the rooftop again, but it was too high. She could only fly about ten feet off the ground. She landed and went back in the freight elevator (still loading soldiers, but now not as many as before) and rode it back to the top.

The man to her right was waiting for her. "That was a trick," she said.

"You're refusing to remember," he said. "It's not because of the dream, it's because of your shame."

Her face flushed. What was she ashamed of?

"You have to turn off the tower." He turned and pointed up to the very top of the shaft, where a blue light blinked and a beeping sound kept pace with it.

"I don't know how to turn it off."

"Yes, you do. You're the one who built it," he said. "I couldn't tell you before. You weren't ready. It's why you're leading this dream. You couldn't sleep. You were tired to death. The shouts, the screams, the Rising Up kept you awake. You built a machine to make you sleep, but it had consequences. It lulled everyone."

This struck at her heart. Franzy could remember her hands on the box, turning the dials, listening to the sounds and refining them.

"They used you, it's true. Before they turned it all the way up, they told you it was to restore order, but in fact you wanted the relief of following orders. So you're responsible for all this." He swept his arms out to the soldiers on the rooftops, all of them staring at her, a vast blanket of faces.

"I'll do it," Franzy said. But she looked up at the aerial antenna and began to wonder why she had to do it. Her eyes swept back to the faces on the rooftops. In the distance she could see a squirming, a rippling of the horizon. "They're coming," she said. "We'll have to fight them."

The woman to her left said, "Don't let that thought come at you. Concentrate and destroy the box."

"The box, the box, the box," the soldiers chanted on every rooftop. The whole city picked it up, and the chant swelled in Franzy's head. She turned back to the tower, which was kind of like an erector set, with lots of metal crosspieces. The tower wasn't as high as she thought and really no harder to climb than a stepladder.

And there was the box, blinking, with a small screen showing a graph. A seagull landed next to the box and eyed her. Then another. Franzy looked up to see the sky covered with birds, all heading towards her.

"Faster!" the woman to her left called from down below.

Franzy looked at the box. Why had she been worried? There was an ON/OFF switch! She reached out to flip it off as the first bird attacked her hand.

"Ignore them!" the man to her right called. "They're butterflies! The sky is filled with butterflies!"

Franzy looked up again, and it was true. The butterflies were in a pattern, as if aligned on a quilt or a sheet, wings quivering, antennae vibrating.

"The switch!" he called out desperately.

Franzy noticed that the sky was half night and half day, divided by a line above the horizon. "If I don't turn it off, what will happen?" she asked. The man on her right kept changing the story. Was he making it all up?

"It's okay, Franzy. It's okay to turn off the switch." His voice sounded slightly different, and she became aware of sounds breaking through from somewhere else.

The beeping grew louder. Franzy's hand rested on the switch. When she removed it, the beep continued, but quieter.

"Why can't *you* turn off the switch?" she asked. "Why does it have to be me?"

"Because you made the switch," he said. "I told you that."

"You told me a lot of things," Franzy said. The line of night and day collapsed a little. The army ranged on all the rooftops looked to her for the next move. This was a strange world, but she was at the center of it. "Why would I make the switch?"

"The switch is for you, so you can break through and go back to the world where you're awake."

She remembered the awake world. It wasn't as good as this world, with all its wonderful surprises. "This is a better world for me," she said.

"Franzy, listen," the man to her right said. His voice sounded familiar now. It belonged to someone she knew in that other world. "You're stuck in a dreamlike state. You can break out of it. All you have to do is make the decision. Pull the switch, Franzy."

Ah. She suspected this was a doctor or someone declaring himself to be a doctor. Someone who wanted her to come to his reality.

"Don't fight us," he said.

"Fight you?" she asked. "Why would I be fighting you?"

"Don't fight the dream," he corrected.

She climbed down from the antenna. All over the rooftops, people watched her. "Who are you?" she asked him. "I think you just tried to trick me."

"It isn't a trick," he said. "We're just trying to get you to wake up, to come back to the real world."

Franzy walked over to the roof and stepped off. As before, she floated down to the ground. The woman she had passed the last time, in the window, waved at her and grinned. "Don't leave us," she said, and then covered her mouth and winked.

Franzy took a glass elevator back to the roof. The line above the horizon shifted up and down, like a window shade. More dark, then more light.

"I like it here," Franzy said. "I like all the possibilities."

"Come back to the real world," the man to her right said. He had a white coat on now. He held a clipboard with sheets of paper with her name on it.

"We'll help you wake up," the woman to her left said. She had a stethoscope around her neck, and surgical scrubs.

"And then what? I can change the world here," Franzy said. With her fingertip she pushed the line between dark and light up and down. *I can do more than that*, she thought. She waved her hand and it rained without getting anything wet. That amused her. There was a different sense of things now, a feeling of change.

Franzy removed her penis. She put it back. She laughed. She couldn't recall ever laughing so fully. She raised her hands, and all the people on all the rooftops laughed as well, a wonderful burst of joy.

"I love it here," she said to the man to her right. "You want this dream to stop, and I don't."

"This is bad for you," the woman to her left said. "You can't really live in a dream. You can't eat or drink or work or love. It's all just an illusion."

Franzy looked around at the moveable sky, at the laughing crowds. She thought about flying again, about making up anything she liked, about the sheer audacity of dreaming.

"This is perfect," she said. "You were wrong to try to trick me into leaving. I don't think you'll ever be able to trick me again."

Her eyebrows rose as a thought occurred to her. "Take these two," she said to the people on the rooftops. "They're balloons, that's all. They never had any power."

The man to the right and the woman to the left began to inflate, their lips pursed. The people grabbed them and tied ropes to their ankles. They spun around slightly, but they couldn't speak because their mouths were swollen shut.

"I want them to be bigger," Franzy said. "Big enough so that I can always look up and see them, and remember that I want to be here, no matter what they send into my dreams."

Franzy jumped with the balloons to the street and tied them to a gazebo in the center of the square. They rose to the second-floor windows, and the woman in the window leaned out and began to throw confetti. Soon everyone was throwing confetti.

The sound of beeping disappeared. Franzy raised the line on the horizon, so it was sunny and warm. There was no tomorrow or yesterday now; there was nothing but peace and pure imagination. She had won. She would always win.

The woman in the window looked down and said, "It's always a choice here, and we choose you!" She blew Franzy a kiss, then turned and pointed to the distance. Franzy saw another army, far off, the air above them glowing pink and red with guns and fire.

"What is it?" Franzy asked. "I thought we were done."

"They're trying something else," the woman said. "With them it's always bread or circuses." She laughed, and her window turned into a balcony. Her dress was short and glittering. She wore little boots, and a feather rose from the hair piled high on her head. Below her, a horse appeared, and she leapt on. As she rode away, she turned and called, "Now, Franzy, now!"

Clowns and acrobats and trapeze artists rushed from buildings all around. "A circus war!" they cried happily. They ran past a sideshow truck with Franzy's image on it. Her right side wore a man's suit and her left side wore a woman's dress. "I am half-man, half-woman," she thought. She could feel a beard on the man-side of her face.

Franzy filled with delirium. They would send other, wilder, smoother dreams at her, trying to win her, trying to trick her.

Carnival music blared and cannons shot out enemies with painted faces. Her heart rose up.

"To war!" she cried. "To war!"

The Apartments

Angela Wilson was walking to the subway station with one of her adult students, after the computer class she taught at night. Erin was in her twenties, walking smoothly and shyly alongside her. It was natural for Angela to ask where she lived. "On Seventh Street in the East Village," Erin said.

"I used to live on Seventh Street," Angela said. "Near what avenue?"

Erin said it was off First Avenue, and Angela thought, how strange. She said, "I used to live off First Avenue. What number is the building?" She looked quickly at her student—why, Erin was older now than she had been when she lived on Seventh Street. So long ago; so very long ago. Such different times. She had gone a little bit aside in her thoughts and almost didn't hear it when Erin said the number of the building.

"Why that was where I lived!" Angela said. "What apartment are you in? I was on the first floor."

"Me too," Erin said and laughed.

It turned out Erin was living in Angela's old apartment.

"How strange," she said. "You're living in my first apartment. How often does that happen?"

"People move around in the city," Erin said. "It must happen a lot."

"But the same apartment?"

They had reached her subway station, so Erin waved and said, "See you next week."

She bobbed down the stairs.

Angela dined out on the story for a few days (it wasn't a big enough story to carry beyond that) and finally said to her friend Lily, "I wonder who's living in my other apartments. That was the first one I had, and now I'm living in" —she stopped to consider her moves around town— "my sixth apartment. Wouldn't it be something if I knew everyone in those apartments? I mean, I know the first one. So there are really only four more connections."

"It's New York," Lily said. "People run into people and find they lived at the same address; it happens all the time. Sometimes even living at the same address at the same time, not even nodding in the hallway, you know what I mean? Timing is the issue in New York; it's everything. You can live upstairs from someone and never meet them. Or the reverse. I'm forever running into old boyfriends I don't want to see."

Angela nodded politely. "Still. She's living where I lived. Maybe even touching the walls where I touched them. Certainly she's touching the door I touched."

Lily raised her eyebrows. "Do you really go around touching walls?"

Angela laughed dutifully, but it was almost as if Erin were walking around in her history, some kind of retroactive ghost.

She had been 19 when she lived on Seventh Street, fluid and impulsive and completely unaware of what was ahead. Each day had dawned bright; people brought weed and crashed in her apartment and crept inside music and nothing would ever end because all of it was just beginning. She had gone to school too, when she lived there, just as her replacement, Erin, now did.

She could picture herself, the self she had been, in that apartment. Opening her window on the first floor, watching the hippies trip down the street and joining them. The world bloomed every day.

❦

Her second apartment was on 10th Street, a loft above an Asian arts store. She was surprised to see that the building was still there, only two stories high, even though most things in the area had been torn down and rebuilt. She rang the doorbell, which didn't have anyone's name on it (continuing an old New York tradition of anonymity, of course). The intercom was fuzzy; she couldn't really identify the staticky voice that snapped out "Yes?" but she said, clearly and slowly, "I lived here thirty years ago, and I'm curious about who lives here now. May I come in?"

"Angela? Is that you?" She froze for a second, unable to place the voice. The intercom was fuzzy; how did whoever it was recognize her? She heard the buzzer and pushed her way in, slowly going up the flight of stairs, wondering who would be there. She heard the door at the top of the stairs open and saw a man lean out and peer down at her. It was Mr. Henshaw, her anthropology teacher from college. She had loved his class.

The surprise of it caused her to slow down just a few steps below the landing.

"It's good to see you, Angela," Mr. Henshaw said, beaming. "Do you want to come in and see what I've done with the place?" He stepped back and waved her in.

He obviously liked the color red. There were red Oriental rugs and nice dark wood furniture and paintings with red splashes. "It's so beautiful," she said, standing and looking around, her head almost swiveling. "Much better than when I lived here. I didn't have much money, so it was mostly used furniture. The only nice thing I had was a small embroidered pillow I loved. It had an elephant on it."

Mr. Henshaw walked across the room and picked something up and turned. "This? It was left behind. I would have thrown it out normally (who knows why people leave things behind?) but elephants are my totem animal." He grinned at her. "I know, a professor with a totem animal." He handed her the pillow.

It was hers. She would have liked to rip it apart. There were things here she couldn't quite process. Her old teacher, her old apartment; what connection did they have? And yet two pieces of her life had met and merged.

"It must have fallen out of a box," she said finally, clutching the pillow. "That's all I can think of. But how did you find this place?"

"You invited me over once, don't you remember? Your English teacher, and one of your friends, as well. It was a snowy night, and you served hot chocolate laced with rum." He closed his eyes briefly. "I can still picture it. Students did invite us over sometimes, of course, but it was usually very dull. A lot of talk about what they intended to do, and we always knew there was very little chance of it." He looked at her intently. "Did you go to Borneo? You insisted you were going to Borneo."

She flushed a little. She had once been to Florida. "I never got around to traveling. I never made much money, so traveling always seemed out of reach."

"You admired Margaret Mead."

"I still do."

19

"Ah."

There was a lapse in conversation. She was a little overwhelmed, still. He made her feel like a student again, like she could disappoint him. "I don't remember telling you that I was moving."

"Your school records always had your address, and I checked once and you had a new one, so I came here. I liked the layout, the openness."

"I don't even remember why I left. In those days, I just got restless and there was always another place." How amazingly open life had been!

"Ah yes," he said. "How easy things are when you're young."

There was not much to add to that, she thought. She was feeling a little awkward. It was hard being in an apartment that had been hers but was not hers; it was odd running into an old teacher so unexpectedly. And it was dizzying to suddenly remember what she'd been, too; what she'd hoped for herself. She had loved anthropology; she had been so impressed with Margaret Mead; she had wanted to explore the world, and be free.

Well, she had been free. But she had not explored the world.

❦

It was some time before she looked up the third apartment. The original idea had seemed like fun, but it had gotten strangely serious. She was aware that she was the teacher of the student living in her first apartment; that she had been the student of the teacher who was living in her second apartment. Such things must have significance. Or they were terribly coincidental, like her friend Lily running into her ex-boyfriends when she did.

She paused in her thought. Or was that, in fact, also significant, and Lily didn't know it?

Her third apartment was in a fourth-floor walkup. There were names on the bells, and she didn't see a name she recognized. That was actually a relief. She had moved in with John here; they had met while she was living in the second apartment and together they had decided between her apartment and his; that's why she had moved. His had been bigger. It was a two-bedroom, with a nice updated kitchen and a little balcony at the back. In fact, she felt quite adult and almost privileged when she'd decided to move in. She had even bought new clothes, nicer things, to signal that she was in some measure more adult. But that had really been a one-shot deal. The clothes were an idea of what she should be; they were not her. She wore them once or twice and then went back to her real clothes, jeans and structured shirts with shoulder pads (those were the times). John had been a wonderful lover, funny in his own way, very caring and open. But he was, it turned out, bisexual, and his greatest loves were all men. She found this out because he met his greatest love two years later. The great love's name was Martin. He was nice; she might have been attracted to him herself, under different circumstances.

She walked slowly up the stairs after she was buzzed in. The walls were beige, and the hallway looked dimmer than she remembered; perhaps it was the residue of all the sadness she'd felt as she learned to her regret just what life with John was all about. A wonderful man; a man who kept trying very hard to love her, because he was also a moral man, a loyal man. But his eye was always—figuratively—looking over her shoulder, looking at the door, waiting for his true love to come through it.

The stairs seemed endless. She remembered how she would dampen her mind, going up those stairs. She had pulled shopping carts up the four flights of stairs, gotten to the top, and wondered if she'd actually pulled them up or if some kind of magic had lifted them. A kind of blindness to the repetition of the stairs. The way she went through life, merely putting a foot in front of a foot, just looking ahead far enough to avoid stumbling. Though of course she did stumble.

She had stumbled with John. Or maybe he had stumbled with her. At the end of it, you think not how stupid you were but how treacherous you were to yourself. If you choose to love someone who is not capable of loving you, who is to blame for that?

She knocked on the door and heard sounds on the other side; someone was home.

A young woman opened the door and stood looking at her. "Yes?"

"I used to live here," Angela said. "I'm visiting all the apartments I used to live in. No real reason. Just to see. The doors I used to live behind." She laughed. For some reason, she felt a little foolish. Why should she feel foolish? It was an interesting thing to do. Going through the steps in her life, the places where she had played out various things. She wanted, very much, to go in and look at this young woman's apartment. She held out her hand. "I'm Angela," she said.

"Oh," the woman said, startled. "I've heard of you. This is so amazing! My father sometimes talks about you."

Angela felt her smile freeze on her face, freeze absolutely solid. "Who's your father?" she asked. She braced herself for the answer.

"John," she said, and added a last name. Yes, Angela's John. The famous John, the great love, the lost love, the man who still came into her dreams, always talking about another man. "He met my mother through you. I know," she added hastily, "I know you were a couple until you left him. It was one of your friends, Bonnie, who came looking for you once, and the two of them hit it off."

"But I didn't leave him," Angela said blindly.

"Oh? You were living here with him, and then you weren't, isn't that right?" the girl said.

"I was living here until your father told me he was in love with another man." She was surprised at herself; this was so blunt. Perhaps it would hurt the girl; perhaps it would jeopardize John's relationship with his daughter. But she had felt a knife to her gut instantly. This other version of the relationship; this possibility—if he had ultimately fallen in love with a woman and had a family, couldn't it have been *her*? Should she have stayed around, fought for him, fought for herself? On the face of it, it was a rotten deal. This girl should have been her daughter.

This maybe-daughter looked annoyed; bit her lip; shook her hair away from her face. "No," she said. That was all she said.

"How old are you?" Angela asked, and the girl said twenty-seven. Angela calculated quickly. Born two years after she left John. "But he was in love with Martin," she said.

"Uncle Martin? He has three kids. With a woman."

Angela nodded (what else was there to do? She was crushed) and said good bye.

She walked slowly down the stairs, slowly out the door, imagining walking back up those steps in some other variation of her life, walking up and calling out to her daughter, walking up and embracing her husband (though she would probably not have married him). But she hadn't wanted children, not really. And she hadn't wanted marriage. Would she have given in? If she'd had an accidental pregnancy, would she have gone through with it?

She hadn't thought to ask where John was. Was he away? Did he live somewhere else and his daughter had taken over the lease? How strange that right now her mind was taken with the girl, not with John. What would she think if Angela turned around and went back upstairs again? Perhaps they would hit it off, and the girl would end up being some kind of surrogate daughter. She would visit often—her old apartment—and they would spend holidays together. And then she remembered, oh, yes, of course, the girl had a family. A father and mother. *John and his wife.*

She shook it off by the time she reached the corner. She was not the kind of woman to brood. What's done is done. Still, there was a little leaden piece of this stuck in her throat.

Apartments four and five were next.

She sat down at her table that night and began to rough in a timeline for her life. What had she done and when had she done it? She had lived in an apartment on St Marks Place, but only for a year and a half. And then shared an apartment in Gramercy Park until she'd found her sixth apartment, where she now lived.

There was no way of avoiding the fact that these apartments were bookmarks in her life. Some she'd spent a very little time in; some she'd spent years in. Aside from John, there were other boyfriends to recall, who stayed for a while and moved on. There was even a cat in one of the apartments (was that number four?). She wasn't really a cat person. Nor a dog person. She should have traveled more. She should have chosen something to dedicate her life to. Not that she really regretted anything. She had meant to have a career and hadn't gotten to it; she had never meant to marry or have children, so that was fine, though this business of John's marriage and John's child bothered her. Had he lied to her? Had he told her what he thought would be easiest for her to hear? She was uncomfortable with this discord between what she had understood and what had happened. Should she really wonder if the bisexual myth was a myth she'd given herself? That she'd heard what John had said ("I'm sorry, but this isn't right for me") and changed it ("I'm sorry but women aren't right for me"). Had she done that?

There was no reason to hurry to her other apartments, to see what tricks and deceits they held.

But, really, how did her student fit into it? With the other apartments, the person living there now was connected to her life at the time she lived there. But the student living in her first apartment was nothing to her. There was no line, straight or jagged, that tied them together.

Unless she was missing something. There might be something obscurely connecting them, some blowoff from her life at that time. It would be easy enough to find this out, so the next time, before class, they fell into step with each other on the way out of the subway. Angela mentioned how interested she had been to find out that Erin was living in Angela's old apartment. It was a curious thing. "So," she said, "how long have you lived there?"

"Oh, a good long time, actually. Maybe nine years."

"Nine years," Angela repeated slowly

"I meant to ask you—you must have lived there shortly after that girl was killed? Or was it before? Everyone warned me about it because I was just about her age. I mean, of course you knew there was a girl who was killed in that apartment?"

"No." Her heart beat a little. She could see the conversation ahead of her, as if it had already happened, or she had imagined it happened. "There was nothing like that."

"Oh, sorry. Well, then, it must have been after you left. There was a girl there—a college student. A guy broke in while she was asleep, didn't know she was there, just wanted to steal some stuff. Anyway, she woke, there was a fight. He had a knife. She died."

"No," Angela said. "No, that was me. I was that girl. But I didn't die."

Erin studied her, frowning, her lips twitching. "What do you mean it was you? The girl it happened to died."

"I didn't die."

"Everyone says she died."

They were both silent. Students filtered into the classroom, taking their seats, opening their notebooks, checking their emails. Angela's head was flashing back and forth between possibilities: maybe indeed there had been another girl, after her? No. She knew that the story was about her. The intruder had broken in while she was trying to fall asleep; he had a knife; she had quietly rolled under her bed.

Why had he looked under the bed? Had she made a noise? A student rustled some papers, and she looked at the clock. It was time to begin class.

After class, she turned to speak to another student, so she could avoid walking with Erin to the subway. She got home in one of those fogs that used to envelop her when she walked up the many flights of stairs to her third apartment. Back home, in her own building, apartment number six, she walked down her own hallway, painted a very pale mint green, and stood before her own door. She placed her hand on the door; she had left fingerprints wherever she had lived; she wanted to make sure she hadn't forgotten to leave them here. She moved her hand all over the door, pressing her hand down, moving over an inch, pressing her hand down again.

Why should she go to the other apartments, numbers four and five? What would she find there? Some strange twist in her own life? Did she want to see who was there if it meant that some little failure on her own part was revealed? Maybe she hadn't done the right things in life, or maybe there was a consequence to every decision she made, some branches that went out to the world, incorporating other people, bending back to her.

Maybe she didn't want to know about them. She had been content; she had almost been happy not to know about John, not to be reminded about her hopes for a career as an anthropologist. Not to be part of a story, for instance, that had her ending up dead.

She wasn't dead, whatever the story said. But she felt a sense of uneasiness, as if someone might be able to convince her she *had* died. An absurdity.

It began to eat at her. Maybe there had, indeed, been another attack on another student after she had left that first apartment? Maybe she had been wrong to think the story was about her, about that night the intruder broke in to steal her meager goods, when she had rolled under the bed and watched as his feet tiptoed around the small bedroom, opening drawers, and then had paused alongside the bed. He had shifted from his left foot to his right foot, once.

And then he had bent down, pulling up the side of the coverlet, peering in at her. One hand held on to the top of the bed. The other hand rested (with the knife in it) on the floor, to give himself balance.

The lighting had been poor and she had meant to keep her eyes closed, so he wouldn't see the whites of her eyes, but she had to know what he was doing. Her breath was ragged and irregular; he could probably hear that.

He had put the knife down and reached for her, but she was too far away and his position was too awkward.

He pulled back, grabbed the knife, and stood up. "Come out," he said. "I won't hurt you."

For years after that, she had dreams where she couldn't scream. Where, try as she might, she opened her mouth and nothing came out.

But right then, at the sound of his voice, she screamed and screamed, not even hearing the sound of his footsteps fleeing, not hearing the side table he knocked over, the lamp that shattered. She stopped when she heard shouting in the hall, pounding at the door, a siren down the street. She crawled out and opened the door and let them in and told them about the man and the knife, the man and the knife.

She had never really seen his face. There was no one to describe. She heard someone say that maybe she had just had a fight with her boyfriend, maybe that was really what had happened, and she had described the knife, over and over again. To convince them that it was all real. A student alone against a man with a knife. That was her story.

She had put up a bolt across the door; she had put gates on the windows. It amazed her to remember that she had lived there for a year after that. She had been very brave.

❦

"How's the apartment research going?" her friend Lily asked, raising her drink in the neighborhood bar. "Does every place look smaller than you remember?"

"Well, yes, maybe," Angela said. "Not so much smaller as paler or something. I actually haven't been paying that much attention to the apartments themselves. Because the people surprise me."

Lily nodded. "I'm not going anywhere near my old apartments." She shrugged. "They're probably still filled with my old boyfriends. And I moved out because I didn't want to see them again, so what would be the point?"

Angela agreed with her slowly. "I'm taking a little break right now. I had a roommate in the fourth apartment who always had too many people visiting. That didn't last long. It was a nice place, but I don't know— do I want to see her or one of her friends living there? I accused her once of taking some money I'd left on the table. What would be the point of going there?"

"No point at all. "

"There'd be some twist. Some kind of irony."

"I hate irony," Lily agreed.

❦

After Lily left, Angela savored a final drink on her own. She was not ready to confront her fourth apartment, but it loomed over her. And the business about John had upset her. She decided she would indulge in a pack of cigarettes on her way home. In fact, that roommate in the fourth apartment had complained about cigarette smoke, forcing Angela to quit. She missed cigarettes.

She felt tipsy on the way home and liked it. She was going to her apartment, where there was no one at all from her past. She had a bottle of wine in the kitchen, and she would have one more glass, and she would smoke her cigarettes and just sit and look out the window, content. Maybe she'd move a piece of furniture. That would be a statement of some kind, not sure what kind.

She opened the bottle of wine and had at least one more glass. She smoked cigarettes and waved them in the air. She moved the sofa to the opposite wall and moved a chair back where the sofa had been.

She was drunk; it was good. She reveled in it. One more cigarette—the ashtray was full, she should empty it first—and then to bed.

Where she fell asleep almost instantly.

She awoke to smoke burning the back of her throat. Her head was spinning and the room was dim. She sat up woozily, blinking, rubbing her eyes. Yes, it was smoke. It was dark. She tried to find the bedside lamp but couldn't. She waved her hands around and found it, knocked it over, and staggered out of bed. She was still mostly dressed. Still half-drunk. Had she left something on the stove? She must have. Had she made tea or coffee or started to cook something? She put her feet over the side of the bed and staggered upright. She was blindingly dizzy, or was it just that she couldn't see much and the smoke was making her cough? She had to get out; she was sure it was best to get out. She stumbled to the doorway.

Only there was no doorway. She slapped her hands on the wall, searching for the doorway. She couldn't make sense of it. There had always been a door there. The door to the living room, to the front door, the way out.

That same jarring feeling that had overcome her when she was back in a former apartment, back in a former part of her life—it returned.

❦

The smoke was getting into the room somehow, so there must be a doorway. A dim light came from across the room and she turned toward it. She crept forward, her arms outstretched. She slammed her outstretched hand against what she thought was the doorway.

Glass. A window! She stood still for a moment, struggling to make it all come together in her head. Her throat was burning, her eyes were burning. She bent over a little; it was better to be close to the floor in a fire; more air. But the window—why was the window there?

No; she was confused. She was thinking of the wrong apartment! It must be the smoke, oxygen deprivation. Whatever it was, she had to concentrate and remember which apartment she was in and where the door was for that apartment.

She was getting dizzy, and it was harder to figure out where she was. She dropped down to the floor and crawled, her hand on the wall. She would find the door eventually; she would have to find it. She crawled slowly. How big was the room? Where was the door? Was she moving or only imagining she was moving? There. There. There was a door.

It was partially open so she pushed it in and moved through, on her hands and knees. And instantly found another wall, only a few feet in. She was gasping. She sat back on her knees, her hands flailing out, left and right, back and forth. Things on the floor, things around her. She fought with them. What could they be? She grasped a piece of it, whatever it was, and it came down and fell over her face. Clothes! She was in a closet!

Where was the closet in relation to the real door? She was getting fuzzier and fuzzier. Which apartment was she in? Why was it so hard to think clearly? Where was the way out? The smoke burned, the air burned, it was hard to breathe; she couldn't breathe.

She made one more try, backing up a little, making sure she continued on her way around the room (she had started to her right, hadn't she? Or was it her left?). She came around a corner and knocked into something and tried to push it but it was too heavy. A bed. She was in her bedroom. She must try to get out.

It was too hard to think, it was too hard to breathe. And she couldn't get out. She crawled under the bed.

And this time, when footsteps came, when a face looked under the bed, when a hand reached in to pull her out, she was gone for good. It was too late. The girl who had died in the first apartment had finally died in the last. The story was done.

Twelve Sisters, Twelve Sisters, Ten

The sisters, all twelve of them, rushed down the corridors, looking at the mirrors, checking on each other. Artemis, short-haired; Bethamis, short-browed; Chloe, red-cheeked; Doloreen, smiling. They wore wide skirts and silk shoes and belts made of crystals. Ellerence wore a velvet blouse; Glorene, satin; Helena, brocade; Ingelise silk. Justinia had feathers braided in her hair.

"Oh, my feet are drunken," Kittilette declared, lifting up half of her mouth in a smile—she had practiced it all afternoon, that half-done smile. "I can feel them getting tipsy."

They were outside now, Bethamis helping Artemis, the eldest, whose thin back was bent, whose fingers were curled.

Ellerence and Fiorence, joined at the wrists, faced each other, sliding into the night. Their faces were taut, strangled with bitterness, joined as they were against their own wishes. All those years of crying out, "To the right!" only to be stymied. Imperious, outraged, they dragged each other sideways. Lotte, the youngest, skipped ahead, her breasts like small gloves; she leapt up and spun, her long hair snapping. Too, too glorious to be sixteen, the youngest, the fastest, the best. She reached the water and curled her foot out of her shoes; behind her the sisters were calling, in muted shouts, in telescoped whispers: "Hold on! Not so fast! Get your hands off me! My turn, mine!"

But she didn't wait for them. At sixteen, why wait for anything? She swayed into the water, sliding in like a snake, ages ahead of Artemis, forty-six if she's a day, brittle and gray and knife-eyed, while *she* was soft as good firm dough.

Her head was under water, hair pulled by waves, and she turned, saw a sister's foot break through and descend, then foot after foot, an ankle, a calf, a hem touched with green, the moon's strong light like a million lamps strung along the lake bottom.

They were all through now, and even Artemis was lighter again, unhumped, her eyes once again lively— they skimmed down the avenue like a cascade.

No one looked back; no one saw a man push his startled face down through the flat of the water; his tongue sticking out, he looked such a fool. He drew back carefully, he had followed so cautiously, he was willing to take his time.

Hired by the Grand Duke their father, that man strangled by daughters, all of them virgins, he swore, he swore; none of them willing to leave him, free him, get married, and be gone. Why won't they marry? Suitor after suitor had come, some of them even clever, some of them even young, but none of them accepted, and half of them sent to their death before they were gone.

Girls. The great disappointment of his life, girl after girl. He'd drowned the first few, but after that he'd let them live, curious as to how far the joke would go, replacing the wives instead. Now he merely wanted to be rid of them. He was nearing 80, and his girls had long ago stopped fearing him, if they ever had. When Martin appeared, young and with insufferable eyes, asking to see his daughters that he might choose one, the old man's heart had surged. This one looked steadfast. He sighed. "They will not marry," he said finally. "None of them."

Martin filled his lungs up with air; a little tail of a smile appeared. "I will choose one and leave her no choice," he said handsomely.

"A tithing of my gold will go to you if you succeed." And with that agreement, the king began to tell all that he knew: time after time he had glimpsed them all in a line in the moonlight, and they had laughed at him when questioned. A line of 12 daughters was not a thing to be handled easily, so he had thought he was mistaken, or that it was some secret women's business, and he cared nothing for that.

"I will find out, first, where they go," Martin said, "and break them of the habit. And the one who thanks me for it will be my wife." He was used to enchantments, and he loved to break them.

Martin combed the countryside for the former wives and found two of them living together in a cottage on the edge of the woods. "I have come to woo your daughters," he said, "and I wish to please them. But they disappear in the moonlight; will you help me win your daughters' love?"

Nigea, the elder, sat inscrutable and unyielding. She said, "My daughters choose their own way; I won't help you deceive them."

"Of course not," Damiel said, but she winked at Martin, one eyelid shutting up and down furtively. "My daughters will be unwed and unprotected for as long as they choose."

Martin thanked them cordially and left, walking slowly, and before long Damiel slipped up behind him and said, "You will marry one of my daughters, the twins, for they need someone to provide for them. Sweet as they are, the world is cruel. Here, this is a reed that will allow you to breathe underwater. Follow them wherever they go, and kill whomever they meet. They won't be free until you do."

In town he purchased a great cape with golden seams and a wide brimmed hat with a single pearl and a knife as thin as a hair. He was bathed and perfumed, and he strode into the rows of daughters as their father's guest, their heads bowing in abbreviated curtsies. They had seen suitors before.

That night they went out as usual in the moonlight, in ones and twos, the youngest racing forward, the eldest lagging behind. "I heard something, I heard something," Artemis said, pulling herself up.

"Some creature in the woods," Justinia assured her, pulling her forward. Already Lotte was in the water, the balloon of her skirt not yet dropping down, and they raced to catch up with her, going too fast for Glorene, who stopped to free her hem from a branch and thought she saw a foot, a human foot with a human shoe, dart back into the shadow. "Ingelise!" she cried to her nearest sister. "I saw a man's foot!"

Ingelise laughed. "I've seen a lot of them, Glorene. Nothing to worry about." She quickly mounted one of the underwater horses that always waited for the sisters. "Hurry, Glorene, the others are miles ahead!"

Martin pushed himself into the water and followed slowly, breathing through the reed, which lengthened and shortened automatically with the depth of the lake.

He heard music, eerie blurred sounds, and began to see a brightness up ahead. He came upon a great house under water and peered in through the windows to a good-sized room with a polished floor and corridors going off like arms.

The dancers sprang up with the beat of the music, raising their arms and stiffening their legs, floating up together, and when they reached the highest point, they spun around together, partnered up, the women twisting their ankles round the men's legs, twirling together.

Martin could make out the eldest—Artemis—now lithe and arching in the dance, and the youngest one, not as good as her sisters and inclined to tangle herself in her clothing. He could see their bare legs, their pointed toes, as they sprang up and slipped back, and his face was grim as he noted how closely they were held, how intimately entwined. All were shameless, save for the bumblings of Lotte, who kept drifting apart from her luckless lover.

He watched as Artemis first, then Bethamis, then Chloe, drew their lovers away from the dance, and window to window he followed Chloe and her lover down a hall to a room, to a bed, dressed in underwater ferns.

He watched, only drawing away when they were done.

At dawn the dancers bade the company adieu, and the sisters mounted their horses and sped back to shore, where they put on their shoes and went home to bed.

Martin took longer, but he too returned above and hastened to the king.

"Your daughters go to a house beneath the water," he said, "where they dance and fornicate and defile your good name."

"All of them?" the king asked.

"All save the youngest," he said, "and that only because she has not yet found a partner. She is the only one I would marry; she is the only one left pure."

"Then the others shall die," the king said.

But an unnoticed servant heard this, and whispered to Artemis, whose crooked spine straightened in fury. "Sisters!" she whispered hoarsely, going from room to room. "We have been betrayed!"

That night eleven sisters went down to the lake, but this time they avoided walking in a line, and the sister who always seemed forgotten—Doloreen—hid behind a tree to see if they were followed. She saw a man's form slip through the shadows and saw it pull the reed from under his shirt and follow.

He slowed down as he neared the great house, and Doloreen hurried ahead of him. She nodded to her sisters and climbed a tree, wrapping her skirt against the trunk where it branched. She watched him as he peered through windows, fingering a knife tied to his side, shifting his weight.

One, two, three of the sisters danced in plain sight. Doloreen could see him shifting, trying to look into the near side of the room, counting four and then five.

Suddenly he felt fingers at his ears and legs. Unseen sisters—two of them, ten of them, how could he tell?—blindfolded him and tied his arms behind, tied his ankles together, careful to leave his reed undisturbed. When he was bound, they put him on a horse and rode far away, and then they tied him to some coral, near a shore he couldn't see, and they left him.

They went back to the ball and gathered. "Sisters," Artemis said, "this is not going to end well. Our father insists on marriage, and he can order our deaths if he chooses. We must consider what to do."

Marriage seemed inevitable if they were to stay their father's wrath. "It's a pity," Fiorence said, "that there isn't a son. He would ignore us entirely then. Too bad one of us isn't a boy." She trailed off, and her eyebrows lifted, and she looked around. The other sisters looked around, too, and began to laugh. And their plan was born.

❦

The very next morning, a cry arose from the sisters' quarters, and Artemis hastened to her father's room with a letter in her hand. "Father, father!" she cried breathlessly, falling at his feet. "That man—Martin—has proven himself a liar and a thief! He has taken Lotte—this is her farewell letter. He has promised to protect her, and wed her—but why would he steal her away then? I'm afraid he will dishonor her and kill her."

"This is shocking," her father said. He sat back abruptly in his chair. "The scoundrel." His bones looked heavier, and he looked weary.

"And liar," his daughter added.

"And liar," her father agreed.

Relieved, the sisters continued with their plan. Lotte waited for them under the lake while the sisters assembled a set of garments, with a cap and jacket, all of which they took with them undersea.

"Come Lotte, it's time," Chloe said as she approached Lotte with scissors.

"Must you really cut my hair?" she asked regretfully.

"Hush, Lotte, you know we must."

"Must you really take away my skirts, and my petticoats?"

"Hush, Lotte, you know we must."

"Must I really wear these clothes?" she cried as they dressed her in a loose shirt, and a vest, and trousers.

"Yes, yes, of course you must," they told her. "And your name is Loren, and you are good and fast and glorious, you know that, don't you? Your father will adore you, and your sisters will be forever in your debt. You'll still have your life here below, Lotte. When you come here you can wear your skirts, and we'll save your hair for you to wear, but look at you now," they said, coaxing her to a mirror.

She looked a good boy—slim and agile. She turned and saw the effect, approving it. "I'm ready," she said, and they mounted up again, eleven sisters and their brother, and rode to shore.

"New shoes," Lotte said, observing a pair along the water's edge.

"And your name now is Loren," they reminded her, and slipped off to their rooms.

In the moonlight, Lotte stood, the last time she would be known by that name. She was the youngest, judged easiest to pass as a boy, and she mourned the loss of the life she knew and began to imagine herself as a boy.

By morning she had it fully in her mind, and she strode off to her father's house—wide strides, sharp impetuous looks, sneers aimed at squirrels and woodcocks.

Loren demanded immediate audience with the duke. "Sir, I am your son," he said. "I only recently found out my mother—your last wife—had been pregnant when you banished her." He bowed deeply.

"My son!" the king cried, leaping to his feet and grabbing the boy by the shoulders to peer at his face. "Yes, yes, I see it. The resemblance is there. A son!" he was beaming. "I shall murder the woman."

"Sire, she is my mother. I would hardly like to mark the day I found my father with the day I doomed my mother." Loren's mouth was firm.

His father blustered. "You're right—I was taken off guard. Old habits. Ah, but this is the future, and just in time. I find myself grown old, my son, and what old man wants to see a legacy of daughters?"

"I have sisters?" Loren murmured in astonishment. "I was raised alone. Having sisters seems like wealth to me."

His father gave a short laugh. "No wealth with this many girls," he said. "But what do they matter? We'll keep them if you like," he said, laughing and slapping his son on the back.

"Dear sisters," the boy said as the sisters swept in at suppertime. He had a faint flush on his cheeks. "Let me first say how pleased I am to meet you, how much I've dreamed of sisters in my barren life. And a father," he added hastily, raising a glass. "To father!" he cried, and they all raised their glasses and cried out cheerfully: "To father!"

At first the old man found a renewed vigor at the arrival of his son, and rode and walked and ate and drank exclusively with him. He noted a bodily modesty about the boy and thought it a shame he had been raised by women, because he had a natural quickness and spirit that a father might have shaped into something fine.

After a week, he felt tired again and went to bed early, his great eyes sunken, his great head weak. Loren waited until he was sure the old man was asleep, then he sped out to the lake, tore off his male clothes, and plunged into the water after his sisters.

Her heart soared as she neared the ball and caught up with the others. "Wait!" she cried. "I hate being a boy!

It's an awfully dull life, with no one to talk to, and father watching over me relentlessly, and shooting at small things unfairly. I'm bound to make a slip, he watches me too closely."

The sisters conferred and agreed that another brother would keep Loren from loneliness, an older brother from a previous wife. And so it was decided that Doloreen—who always complained she was overlooked, anyway—would join Lotte—or Loren, they corrected themselves.

The next morning the sisters reported that Doloreen was ill, and the day after that no better. On the third day the sisters begged to send her to her mother, a noted herbalist, and her father consented. What did he care, really, if the house had one less girl?

Within a week, the carriage returned with the news of Doloreen's death—and more to the point, a young man with a happy stride gave him the news in a mournful voice that ended with the phrase, "Imagine my sorrow to see her, sir, my sister."

"Sister," the king said thoughtfully. "So your mother re-wed?"

"Ah no sir, never. She said her happiness was complete as long as she could keep *one* of her children by her side, and that was me. It is only by my sister's death that I learned how to find my father. Sir, my name is Nicholas." He bowed, his hand nearly touching the floor.

"Another son!" the old man cried in wonder. "How awful these women are and what a good thing I didn't kill them all. Come closer, let me look at you. Yes, the face says it. So like your sister, you could be twins!" He shook his head in wonder. "You have a brother, you know, a younger brother."

"And sisters, I understand."

"That too," the father agreed, and took him off to meet Loren. "Two sons," their father said, marveling.

"Who knows," Nicholas said, winking to Loren. "Who knows—there may be more."

"I will have to change my will. It will all go, of course, to the first born son." He waved his hand around the estate.

"That's right," Loren said, startled. He looked at Nicholas, who grinned to himself, his eyes wandering around the house and the grounds, his eyebrows arching, his chest swelling.

"What difference does it make?" Artemis asked Loren later on. "You or Nicholas—it's all the same.'

"It's not the same," Loren answered. "He's not like me, I saw his eyes. He's greedy."

For Nicholas was quick to claim things, going around with his father and discussing changes. He wanted trees to come down so he had a better view from his window; he wanted a new stable built for horses, which he rode until they foamed. He was invited away for weekends and came back boasting of his popularity. And he intended to marry.

"Marry?" Artemis gasped.

"Oh only in name," he assured her. "Some pretty young thing without a clue in her head but with a good pedigree." He glanced at his shocked sisters. "That was the plan, wasn't it? What's the point if I don't marry?"

"But," Bethamis said carefully, "if you marry and you die, the place goes to your wife. We'd be out on our ears."

"Oh don't worry," he said indifferently. "If I married without issue, the place would go to Loren."

43

At which Loren's teeth began to show, and a plan fell in place in his heart.

❦

Nicholas ordered a party upon the water, with boats and lights and musicians and singers. People leaned over the edge of the boats and pointed below them, where other lights and dancers appeared.

"Reflections," Nicholas said lazily. "Just reflections. Look," he said, and tossed a stone into the water. Everything broke apart and his guests laughed.

Bethamis leaned over the side of a small boat, which she'd taken out herself, and she peered down below, where she could see that a rock had landed on a dancer, who was stumbling back inside.

"See that?" her brother said, pointing to a rocky area. "I intend to build a pavilion there, with gondolas and floating beds." He laughed and drank another draught of port, which he had grown to love and which his father spoiled him with. His voice was loud and booming, and the party lasted for days, during which Artemis limped, during which Ellerence and Fiorence faced each other without remission, and the other sisters, too, chafed at being kept from the lake. Nicholas had the house overflowing with guests; they couldn't take the chance on being seen.

But the angriest was Loren, who saw how arrogant and profligate his brother was. Nicholas frequently forgot to introduce him, even, as if he were one of the sisters, and not a boy. Loren grew angrier and angrier, and went to his father.

"He's not your son, sir," he said. "I have seen him naked, and he has a tail, I've seen it, he's the devil himself. I'm sorry to grieve you."

"A tail!" the king said, astonished. He had heard of beings with tails, there were stories everywhere about it, and he sent for Nicholas at once. "Disrobe," he demanded. "I know what you are!"

Nicholas was alarmed. Disrobe and expose himself to be a woman after all? How had his father heard this? He cast his eyes around the room, which contained his father's courtiers and lawyers. "I am too modest," he said finally. "Raised as I was by women."

"Strip him," his father ordered, but Nicholas ran away and was gone.

The king turned his attention to Loren, who stood near him. "And you?" he asked. "What are you?" His eyes were sharp and unloving

"I am only your son," Loren said weakly, his heart pounding. He took a step closer to the door—a movement his father noted with an intelligent eye.

"You have the choice—leave without question now or be subject to the test," the king said.

And Loren fled.

"Call my daughters," the king said, "however many there may be."

"Father," said Artemis, entering quickly, "father, we're here."

"I know who you are," their father said. "Known you since you were born, and only lately have I discovered the value of a girl grown at home. Never before has a duke left his worth to a girl; it has ever been sons. But I am grand duke, and I decree: from this time forward, it all goes to daughters, who shall rule it together. Sons are the very devil," he said.

When their father began to weaken from his final illness, the servants were released with gold coins filling their hands, and the oldest girls went off to return as men and wed their sisters. A great ceremony was held, and neighbors from high and low were called in to rejoice. The sisters and their husband-brothers danced all night and into the next day. Occasionally, a tradesman would murmur, "That one there—do you see it? Bent over like that, like the eldest that was. Do you see it?" but people were inclined to fill their glasses up again and join the merrymaking. And after that, the blissful couples shut the door on all outsiders and ran their lives as husbands and wives for the sake of the servants, who all went to bed early and never saw the sisters stepping into the waters or returning at dawn, happily spent.

How to Be a Foreigner

"Stand still," Maria said, annoyed. "Stand still *on the ground*."

Because that was the one thing that seemed to be the hardest for the alien to remember.

Maria had convinced it to stop being green, to get rid of the extra arms, and to get its face into a shape that resembled a human face. It was a little too bulbous (obviously the way the alien saw Maria's face, how insulting), and the skin color was a little too consistent. Kind of PhotoShopped.

The alien got a patient look on its face. It was starting to pick up mannerisms. Her mannerisms? She frowned; the alien watched her.

Maria was determined to get this going right; she was big on organization and positive reinforcement. "Good for you!" She smiled heartily. It smiled back.

"Now about your clothes—" This was going to be harder. She could pass it off as a foreigner rather than an alien if it fit the local idea of what a foreigner looked like. People here were convinced that foreigners meant illegals. It would be better if the alien didn't look so—so—fashionable. So ahead of things. So much the avant-garde.

Unless it was Italian? Could she get it to look Italian? The locals had seen Italians on TV, she was sure of it. She went to the Internet and brought up various examples. She wanted modern ones, but not from New Jersey, she decided. The locals might have relatives in New Jersey, for all she knew, and they might ask technical questions.

She was getting side-tracked. She looked at her visitor with renewed focus.

The alien, with its one-tone skin and its indelicate features, wore a kind of silky tunic over two sets of leggings, one ending at the feet, one ending below the knee. The colors were muted, but the clothing caught the light and seemed to shimmer. The tunic had a band around the hips, emphasizing a strangely attractive tubular waistline. Two thin scarves were draped at the neck and curved down across the breast and to the back, like bandoliers. A stiff, almost pleatherlike collar lay flat along the neckline. A band ran from the forehead down to the back of the neck, where it scooped out a little bit. Soft boots. Loose bracelets of tight beadwork at the wrists. She thought she saw a sixth finger, and then it was gone. Perhaps it was hanging from the beadlike chain that dangled where a designer would have put a pocket. Because a few things did dangle from it, and Maria was determined not to look at them too closely.

This alien had style. Maria licked her fingers and wetted her own eyebrows, as if to enlarge them, and the alien did so as well—and its eyebrows were thick and had an interesting arc to them, not so much startled as slightly dumbfounded. Or, yes, startled and slightly disapproving. It didn't matter. The more Maria saw, the more she was convinced that this look would catch eyes, and instead of trying to have this alien fit in, which was her original thought, now it made more sense to try to promote it in some way that might reflect well on her.

Because, after all, she had not killed it when it plunked right down on the top of her car parked in her driveway, which she'd been thinking about washing. Fell just like blue ice from an airplane.

She had looked up immediately but saw only a vapor trail.

The creature had been slightly stunned. It sat up on the roof of her now-dented car, and looked at her.

It had one extra eye, slower than the others. After the alien looked at Maria intently, the third eye closed slowly and began to erase itself.

It didn't matter, that part didn't matter. The alien made no threatening moves, and although Maria could have shot it—she was a good shot when she went out for skeet—she didn't. That made her responsible for it, but also meant she deserved something in return.

The alien emitted strange little beeps. Maria mimicked them a few times, but who knew what she was actually saying? So she spoke in clear, educational sentences: "I would like you to come with me very nicely, not making a problem of any kind, while I figure out what to do." She waved her arms around in an effort to help. It seemed cooperative, with the disappearing eye and all; perhaps it would learn to speak. She could go with the Italian idea. Though if she ran into an Italian....

Some island in the Mediterranean, then. Be vague. There are a bunch of countries in the Mediterranean; if they ran into anyone Mediterranean, it could always be an island off some other country's coast.

Maria had a habit of fingering objects as she thought, and the chainlike thing at the alien's pocket level had caught her eye and, inadvertently, she was holding on to it. She suddenly jerked herself upright and dropped it, alert to a movement from the alien's arms.

It took off the chain and handed it to her. "Took off" was perhaps too benign. It pulled it with a little force, a little tug and yank. Maria would have thought it would unhook, if it was an accessory.

In turn, the alien touched Maria's necklace. It was not particularly meaningful, so she took it off and handed it over.

Then, compulsively, Maria touched the wrap around its neck, which it removed and then it touched Maria's sweater, which she removed and then touched one of its tunics....

Stripped, they stared at each other. The alien touched Maria's breasts; she touched some pouchlike things under its arms (no doubt that explained the particular drape of its scarves). There was a moment or two of processing, then the alien handed Maria back her underwear and she handed it back its leggings, and so on and so on.

When they were done, the alien climbed back on top of Maria's car and looked up to the sky.

With hope? Was it wishing to go home? She supposed it was.

But then there was another thump, and next to the alien was another alien.

Maria cursed herself. She had looked away, really just for the briefest time; she had looked at her watch, and she had missed how this had happened.

The two aliens leaned together and looked at her.

And then there was another alien, just like that. She was looking at them even as she heard the thump, so she never actually saw the moment—perhaps it was too fast?—when the next one arrived. Or the one after that.

In all, there were five, all of them beautifully dressed according to her own standards. The shades of the clothing varied, and she admired certain combinations more than others. A few had more scarves or more of the pleatherlike bands. The newest arrivals had three eyes and an extra arm, but as they looked around, checking the earlier arrivals, they quietly disposed of the extra things and matched skin color and numbers of organs and appendages.

They climbed down off the car, and all but one of them rose off the ground. Then they noticed that the first one stood on the earth, and they followed suit.

They surrounded the car and began to touch it.

She was beginning to think it was something like a bus tour.

"You're not taking my car," Maria said firmly, but she was outnumbered. They climbed into the car, leaving the driver's side empty, and the first one—she could tell it was the first one—grabbed her by the hand and pulled her around to the driver's side. "Well, just this once, but I decide where to go," she said grumpily.

In fact it felt good to have a load of aliens politely asking to be shown the sights.

She took the long way into town, passing a stand of lodgepole pines (her favorite), which caused the aliens to crane their necks and make their sounds. They passed some forsaken shacks with broken things in the yard. They passed a school with flagpoles and fences.

They came into town with its blinking lights and its parked cars and lots of people getting in and out of cars.

The aliens were very interested in the people and kept pointing and beeping.

She took them to the general market, thinking that this would be the best cross-section of culture. Two of them went down aisles looking at boxes and cans and jars, examining the photos and drawings on them. The rest went with Maria to the clothing section, picking things up and holding them against each other. They fingered the fabrics.

A group of teenagers came in; it was obviously after school, something Maria would have avoided if she'd thought about it.

But the girls clumped together and started hooting at the foreigners.

"What is that?" one of them squealed to Maria.

"He's French," she answered. "You know about the French."

"He's French!" the girl screamed, and the other girls joined in.

The aliens froze. They looked at the girls in their tiny tee shirts, their shorts, their painted nails and freeze-dried hair. One alien went over and tentatively touched an earring, causing more screaming.

The cashier called out, "If you girls can't stop scream-ing, you'll have to leave the store."

"He's French," the ringleader shouted, and the girls proceeded to giggle, then they turned and left the store.

The French aliens beeped to each other rapidly. They put down the clothes they'd been looking at. The ones who'd been looking at food didn't have anything in their arms, either.

Maria naturally headed for the counter and the ca-shier, since she had a bag of sugar. There were some old, sad tourist items on the counter—some keychains, postcards, maps, and a few snow globes.

The aliens liked one snow globe very much. It was a replica of a cabin and a cactus and a coyote howling at nothing in particular. The aliens kept upending the globe and beeping. Did they like the snow? Didn't they have snow? Or did they think that shack and that cactus were representative of life on earth?

Two others conferred together near the plate glass window, looking at people in the street. Maria watched with them and saw people in sweat pants, loose jeans, loose, torn tees or sweatshirts, and sneakers. The men were grizzled; the women were dowdy. She looked at her aliens, all impeccably fashioned. One little girl passed by with leggings under her dress, and they got excited. Maria felt a little embarrassed for her town.

They handed her the snow globe, and she paid for it. They all went straight to the car and climbed in.

She thought they looked away any time she looked at them in the car. "Tell them we have great health care," Maria said weakly. Then she remembered that wasn't true for aliens.

She took them back to her place, where they all got back up on the car and, one by one, reversed the thump and disappeared.

They took the snow globe.

After a day or so, nothing happened, and Maria felt the need of marking the aliens' visit. Plus, of course, they might come back.

She wasn't sure they would; she thought perhaps there was nothing much to see. Had they liked the lodge-pole pines? Hard to tell.

There had only been one thing that she was certain they liked, so she found another snow globe and took photos of it stark against the best fabrics she could find—and one at the base of the lodgepole pines—and took the photos to the print shop and made postcards on glossy stock and on matte.

She seeded them around town, at the market and at the movies, and stood a rack at the end of her driveway, where she waited for a tell-tale thump. In the meantime, she was practicing tying a scarf a dozen different ways.

She knew how picky the French could be.

What They See on Nox

Alta and Billy Bedeene were skeptical about the stories concerning the planet Nox; they were practical, open-minded people, not easily spooked. An agreement with any sentient life on Nox would secure mineral rights for AdAstra Mining and Minerals, but all attempts to communicate had failed. The pay was decent, and there'd be a nice fat bonus if Alta and Billy were the ones to make the linguistic breakthrough with the natives.

It was clear from the moment they landed and introduced themselves that everyone already on Nox had nerves. "Always walk together," they were told by the intake facilitator when they disembarked. "You'll feel better until you adjust to the constant twilight. If you walk alone, sometimes you dissociate."

"Dissociate?" Alta asked. "I know hallucinations have been reported, but I'm not clear: does everyone get the same kind of hallucination? Can we prepare ourselves for it?" She had clear eyes and a high forehead, and she always seemed to be raising her eyebrows to emphasize both.

The facilitator hesitated. "I can't really talk about it. No predisposition—that kind of thing. How could we be sure it wasn't simply the power of suggestion?"

"I'm not that suggestible," Alta said. Billy added, "She really isn't." He radiated confidence. "And neither am I," he said, nodding for emphasis.

They were given instructions for coping with the environment. "The pills help a lot," their facilitator said, "especially for sleeping, since there's no difference between day and night here. I recommend the pills. A large moon this week, so it's a little brighter than usual, but it makes the inhabitants—the citizens—a little…" He cleared his throat. "Iridescent. There's a vid in your room going over some of the ways we've tried to communicate with them so you don't duplicate efforts. We have good food here—efforts at keeping us happy—and we get together for group discussions at noon, 4 p.m. and 8 p.m. (we keep earth time) to go over encounters and reactions."

"Therapy," Billy observed.

The vid in their room told them that the Noxites tended to follow people around, "white shadowing" them. The first team had tried to talk to them, had allowed some of them into the living quarters, but these silent, hollow-faced, open-mouthed, wispy creatures made everyone jumpy. Driving them out again had been difficult because they felt a little like air; you grabbed them with your hand, and they sort of collapsed within your hand, so you let go and they rippled away. It had taken a day to be sure they were gone, and from that point on, no one was allowed to let them inside again.

They had no identifiable food source; there was no water; no one had found evidence of shelter; no one had caught them sleeping or shitting or copulating or accumulating valuable objects. They didn't act like sentient beings of any kind.

❦

"So why does everyone think they *are* sentient beings?" Alta asked Ruby, a habitat engineer who sat at their table in the cafe for lunch the next day.

Ruby bit into her sandwich. "That's what they look like," she said. She was curiously neutral, as if holding something back. "So everyone treats them as if they're sentient beings like us."

"You don't think they are like us," Alta said, encouraging her.

"Not like us, no," she said. "But that's a lot of territory, isn't it?"

"Ah," Alta said.

Billy raised the possibility that the citizens weren't the problem, and the teams weren't the problem. "Maybe there's a chemical or a dust or bacteria that makes us see them. Some kind of psychotropic…"

"Everybody seems sane or normal or routine enough…."

"Until they're not." Billy nodded vigorously. "You know, if you're nuts, you're not necessarily nuts *all the time.*"

"Meaning, I suppose, that if you're sane, you're not sane all the time?" She looked at him with amusement.

❦

It was a thrill to finally see the inhabitants (whom they'd been told to refer to as "citizens") up front and personal. They had been advised not to use the words *ghosts*, *ghouls*, *specters*, or any equivalent phrase—and it was all too easy to see why.

Alta and Billy fell silent, watching the citizens drift toward them as they stood outside the complex in the dusty landscape. They were tall and billowy, with sheetlike arms and legs that were a little indeterminate in the Noxite dusk. Their heads were gauzy with shadowy eye sockets and nose holes and mouths that were perpetually open and moving. Their arms always seemed to be moving, too—warning, entreating, reaching—and their appearance made every gesture seem significant. The half-light didn't help. Although it never went completely dark on Nox, it always seemed about to. The light also threw shadows that a worker sometimes stepped over, thinking it was solid. Or they tripped over a rock, thinking it was a shadow.

"Do they frighten you?" Alta said in a low voice.

Billy, as always, took his time to decide. "They *look* like ghosts," he said finally. "But that doesn't make any scientific sense. Should I think they're human souls who couldn't move on? Spirits with unfinished business?" He shook his head. "Magically transported here? Why?" He was proud of his skepticism. "I wonder what we look like to them."

They were congregating like flies on pie, Alta thought, so she said, "Food. I bet we look like food." She held her hand up to forestall him, but he answered anyway, "They don't eat."

"I know. I read the report. I wonder if they're a kind of air plant. Or if there are microorganisms they feed on. Or radiation or light waves or something. Whatever they are, they're not like us at all."

Despite this, they tried a variety of things that people like them would understand. They threw balls, did mime, drew pictures in the dirt, and once, famously, Alta peed in front of them. They made photos of the creatures and projected them onto screens to show them; they made photos of themselves, which they projected and stood in front of. In all cases, the creatures flitted by, or clumped together, or did whatever it was they always did silently; there was nothing that could signal progress.

"We could throw a tarp over them. Just to see what would happen," she said at one of the general meetings all employees were required to attend. Like AA meetings, Billy observed.

"I'd help you with that," Lukas, an engineer, said. "I'd like to round them up. Like little guppies. Scoop them up. Let them see what it feels like."

"Like what feels like?" Ilsa, the resident shrink, asked.

"The way they stare at us," Lukas said. "Watching us. *Haunting* us."

Alta groaned internally. The shrink said they were projecting their own feelings about death and afterlife onto the citizens; that the ghostly appearances elicited all their childhood fears, but despite Lukas' knowing nod, it was obvious he didn't get it. A day later, Ruby told them that Lukas had been sent home.

"So what do you think?" she asked Billy. "Any theories?" They were putting poles into the ground and hanging sheets with cutouts for faces on them. They'd been having an interesting time, despite the irritations of not having solved the communication problem.

"We could start by figuring out what ghosts really are," Billy said. "For analytical purposes, I mean; what is it that people encounter when they claim they've seen a ghost."

"Well—psychical energy? Leftover emotional or traumatic debris?"

"So. Point one is that emotions are always part of the ghost experience. Fear, love, loss, guilt. And the emotions don't come from the ghost." He pursed his lips. "So, simply, ghosts *attract* emotion?"

Alta hung up another sheet and nodded. "Every ghost story I've ever heard relied on the people who saw them getting scared. Yes," she said, "if a ghost wasn't greeted with terror, the ghost would have to take his bag of marbles and go home. And I think we're making it worse by assuming that we can't go anywhere without a companion. Aren't we sending out signals that come back at us amplified?"

"But the first crew didn't know anything, did they? And look what happened to them." They were finished with their fake ghosts; they stood back and admired them. The citizens drifted around and away.

Billy was a heavy sleeper, so Alta had no doubt she could slip away at night just to see what it was like being out alone. There wasn't much in the way of security; she simply walked down the corridor and out the door.

The Noxites were clustered haphazardly, as usual. They swirled gently around her. Their sheetlike clothing drifted out and back, their arms rose and fell as if they thought they were flying; their mouths were in their perpetual Os of distress.

She stopped, simply to get them to stop, which they did soon enough, some of them hanging near her, draping themselves in the imagined wind.

"Every being that I know of desires something," she began in a quiet, reasonable voice. "Every being. Do you have children? I haven't seen any smaller versions of you." She glanced around the drifting creatures. One of them lifted a hand and came toward her.

She was startled. She winced; she moved abruptly back, causing a new eddy of drifting Noxites. The one heading for her adjusted its hand and reached out for her face, her cheek or jaw, she wasn't sure because she moved again, sidestepping it as it approached. Her heart was beating rapidly.

But while she hesitated, it happened.

It was like a touch of cloth, like a spiderweb, like a feather or a piece of hair. And the instant it happened, Alta felt a combination of emotions—longing, pleasure, regret. There was nothing frightening or horrible about it; it was gentle and yearning. Probably no one else had allowed themselves to be touched, but she had. She had just communicated with a citizen. Or been communicated with? She decided it didn't matter.

❦

"Billy," she said loudly, shaking her husband awake. "Billy! I met them! I communicated with them!"

Billy blinked rapidly and frowned. "What? Here? They're here?"

"No, listen. I went out. I wanted time to look at them without everyone being so… so hypervigilant. They're perfectly okay," she said. "They communicate by touch." She laughed quietly. "Everyone's so freaked out; that's why no one noticed. Too scared to let them touch. That's all it is! Billy, we'll get the bonus."

Billy was now sitting up, expressions of doubt and hope flickering across his face. "What did they say?"

She pulled herself back slightly. "Well, not much. Not yet. I just said hello; I really couldn't discuss the contract right away, could I? I just said hello."

She sat down on the edge of his pallet. "It was a tremendous feeling, Billy. I felt connected, in a strange way.

Not understanding a thing, but peaceful. But I have confidence that this was the breakthrough we've been looking for. It's definite."

"But no words about the contract," Billy pointed out. He was looking at her thoughtfully.

❦

In the morning she decided to tell Radisson, the director of the station; after all, this was a breakthrough, wasn't it?

And Radisson told the support staff, the genius guys, so they could be prepared for further developments.

And one of the geniuses told Radisson he had some news.

"I've been working on something that might change things a bit," the genius, Filper, said. "It's a visual device. It will show us what the citizens really look like. They cross over into the lower range of the spectrum," he explained. "I think that may be troubling to our brains—the fact that they shouldn't be visible but are, because they waver on the boundary."

"Then they're *real*," Radisson said thoughtfully. "Yet you try to touch them and they're not substantial."

"They may not be where we think they are because of the wavelength shift. An optical illusion."

"So they are sentient beings," Radisson said. He felt a little disappointed with Filper.

"Well."

"Well what?"

"They emit light waves. So do rocks, by the way. And trees. And water. Not necessarily proof of organic life, though organic life would have to emit them." He paused. "Organic life as we know it," he added hastily.

"This isn't getting us anywhere."

Filper straightened up, looking chagrined. "My fault. The point is, we can create a lens to correct the visible light shift." He gestured to his workspace. "I'm almost done with the prototype."

Radisson walked over and picked up a gray-colored lens. "This?" he asked. "Have you tried it yet?"

"Not outside. Just on photos or videos. I never go out—you know that." Certain staff members, like the doctors, shrinks, and engineers, were required to stay indoors, away from the ghosts, to stay psychologically clean.

Radisson put it down. "When can I try it?"

"You'll try it?"

Radisson frowned. "I've been here the longest, and they don't seem to affect me. For a first try, I'm the logical person."

Filper shrugged. "Tomorrow, then. I'm just making them into glasses, just adding frames. We'll work on the design if this is the way to go."

"Tomorrow," Radisson agreed.

The special glasses worked—or, at the very least, the glasses changed what Radisson saw, shifted the wispy ghostly forms into something else. As he stood there, a sense came over him of lost chances, of life run out too quickly, of regrets and refusals. He could not for a moment think how he had ended up here, nor if it mattered.

The citizens pooled around him; he braced himself for them, sometimes looking at them full-face and then glancing away to quiet his nerves. And then, finally, he saw something in them—in one of them—that cut him deeply. He stumbled; he took off the glasses; he stared with a stricken face and a shaking heart; and he went back carefully to Filper.

"These are no good," he told Filper. "Just sort of made those creatures thicker. And—" here he licked his lower lip—"made me feel uneasy. Unsteady. Like everything else was out of focus. Like my eyes were arguing with me. One of them was crying—"

"I don't think they can cry." Filper's tone was a little sharp.

Radisson stared at him hatefully. Filper dropped his gaze, picked up the glasses, weighing them in his hand. "I'll check it out. I'll make some adjustments. My numbers must be off."

Radisson took a deep breath. "No," he said. "I wasn't clear. Your glasses work. But what they show is unbearable. Destroy the glasses, I don't want anyone going off the deep end because of them."

Filper raised his eyebrows. "What was so terrible? What did you see?"

"Just destroy them," Radisson said.

"Of course." He slipped the glasses into the waste bin and watched Radisson walk away. Then he took the glasses out again and began to fiddle with them.

Filper told Alta about his glasses. "I modified them so we can see what the citizens truly look like—they're just slightly outside the normal wavelengths we see, that's why they look the way they do to us. Not quite in our register."

"Ah!" Alta cried. "So that's it. We basically just don't *see* the same way?"

"I don't know what they see. I do know that Radisson tried it and then told me to destroy the glasses. So if you want to give it a go, you've got to be quiet about it."

"What did Radisson see?" she asked.

"He wouldn't tell me. Of course, he's been here the longest of all the people who've gone outside; maybe it just caught up with him. Most people who go outside get affected eventually."

She loved the idea of being stronger than Radisson. She had faith in herself and pocketed the glasses and hurried outside.

She walked in one direction and found geologists cracking rocks. In another direction a small pre-fab was being assembled. She went farther away, walking as fast as she could without attracting attention, until the compound was far behind her.

She stood still and waited. No one had followed her; no one was here. She could see citizens as usual in their clumps of three or four. They had seen her and were gradually heading toward her, where they stalled and accumulated, not quite touching her.

She put the glasses on and felt her eyes cross as she tried to get the world around her in focus. With a final effort she steadied her gaze on the dusty ground, on the small rise of rocks, and then she raised her head and saw them.

Some had their hands extended, reaching out; some clasped their hands as if pleading. Her eyes, now clear, scanned them. Her eagerness fell away. Their faces were human faces—all yearning, appalled, and needy. Their bodies, their clothing—all human. Their hands were human hands. There could be no doubt; they were human.

She dropped her eyes. She raised them. Some of the creatures were coming toward her, their faces twisted with supplication. She straightened herself mentally and moved toward them, saying, "Hello. My name is Alta." She tried as hard as she could to keep her voice from shaking.

"You look just like us," she said. "Not merely human, but earthly. And, really, I can see styles of clothing that were around when I was a child. And your faces…some of you." She paused, her own face tightened with concern. "I would say you look familiar."

Her eyes rolled past one face, then came back to it. She blinked; looked away; looked down; and became quiet. Her body was still as she tried to make sense of what she saw.

She saw herself.

Heading toward her, mouth open in a silent scream, hair shorter than her hair was now and quite gray—the eyes madly beseeching, the hands opening and closing in a twitchy, unhappy way—it looked like her; it *was* her: dead. The ghost of herself, the future, end-of-the-line of her own particular destiny.

And the other faces began, one by one, to be recognizable, too. Old aunts, grandparents, neighbors, teachers of classes she hadn't taken; what were they doing, mixed up with the ghost of herself, the dead future of herself? Her ghost was coming toward her.

She turned and stumbled. The damn glasses were interfering with her spatial perception. She took them off; they were preposterous. How could she have seen what she did? She kept her eyes ahead, her back to the ghost of herself behind her, perhaps beseeching her still. She would have no more to do with them, with the "citizens"—a ridiculous term, a pretense; dangerous to think of them so nicely. They were horrifying. She hurried inside, unwilling to admit to Billy that she had been so frightened. So wrong and so frightened. She stood in the hallway, summoning up her strength. After a bit, she held the glasses out and turned them to and fro, thinking.

❦

"Explain how you got this to work," Roger, Filper's father, said. He was looking at a pair of Filper's special glasses. Not the ones Alta had said she'd lost; Filper had had to make a new pair. Filper didn't believe the business about losing them, but the way she'd avoided his eyes made him wonder what she'd seen. What was everyone seeing? He decided he had no choice; he would have to wear the glasses himself and see what was happening.

So he had moved his workroom outside into an unfinished shed, and he was delighted, the very next day, to have his father tap him on the shoulder and say, "Surprise! Guess who's here." It was gratifying: his father had come out for the chance to get the big bonus, but he also said he wanted to see what his son was doing. He'd heard things, he said. He'd heard great things.

"It's the arm of the glasses," Filper explained. "If you look closely, you'll see a little sensor at each end; it resets the visual perceptions. The brain mapping is pretty much the same in everyone, and I'm only touching a very small point anyway, no damage done. And then voilà, a whole new world." He held out a pair of glasses. "You can try them, if you want." Filper grinned at his father and held out the glasses.

Roger waved them off. "It's wonderful, when you think about it. A bridge to communicate with a new species.

And my son did that. You have no idea how impressed I am. And proud."

Filper glowed. He hung his head slightly, modestly. "They're not really ghosts, you know. I thought at first they were at the edge of our visual spectrum, but now I think they're just an unusual form of static electricity. We create them by moving around so much."

"Static?" Roger asked. "Charged particles? Well—when you think about it—we're all charged particles, aren't we?"

A remark that made Filper like his father even more.

"So what did you see?" Alta asked Radisson when she finally tracked him down. He looked at her without answering, so she shrugged and said, "I saw myself, my future, aged self, dead and holding out arms to get me." She shivered. "I've been trying to force myself to go out again, but it's hard. So what did you see? Everyone knows you saw something. They say you want to go home."

The way she said "go home" was deliberately challenging, but she'd gotten Radisson's attention. "I told him to destroy those glasses," he said. His mouth curled.

"Well, actually, he's giving them out as fast as he can make them. There's a sign-up sheet outside the cafeteria. I know I still have my pair—I told Filper I threw them away because I was so upset." She gave a short laugh. "But I kept them. I want to see what happens if I put them on again. But, you know, I'm a little reluctant to go out there again and look. What about you? What did you see?"

He took his time. "Someone I once loved very dearly; she died after we separated." His eyes looked away from her. "She died because we separated."

Filper worked tirelessly; he made glasses and tried them on before putting them out for collection. His father stood beside him, encouraging him. "You were always the smartest kid in school. In the neighborhood," he said. "I knew you were smart; that was a given. But what I took pride in was how just you were. You never hurt anyone in your life."

Filper stopped for a moment and let his father's remarks roll over him. His father had, once upon a time, seemed to be distant from him. Age, time to think, a new way of looking at life; whatever it was, his father's words meant everything to him. He took his happiness and bent over his glasses, intent on making them better. His father would never cease to be proud of him.

Billy wanted Alta to get rid of her glasses, but she wouldn't. She told him, "I have a feeling that if I could see the first one I saw—"

"The dead you?"

She flushed in annoyance. "—I have a feeling I would understand what's going on."

"Well," Billy said. "I don't know why you would think that. It's an illusion of some kind; it doesn't *mean* anything. It's hitting some part of your brain, that's what Filper said. You wouldn't fall for it, normally. How do you feel?"

She glared at him. She understood the implications. Firing up parts of the brain, maybe firing up parts they hadn't anticipated. But she felt perfectly normal; it was a normal human desire to see a curiosity. The curiosity of herself. What person wouldn't be interested in that?

But then Radisson was officially listed as missing, and Billy began to watch Alta closely.

℗

While the whole place was searching for Radisson, rumors began to circulate that the citizens were probably just static. How was anyone supposed to get *static* to sign the mining lease? Static couldn't harm Radisson, so he had simply wandered off and would eventually be found. All of this contributed to Alta's gloom. Plus, she wondered if there was a *meaning* to what she'd seen; was she dying? No one else had seen themselves. Radisson's disappearance began to seem important in some consequential way; what happened to him would happen to her.

Finally she told Billy she was going to find Radisson, and he insisted on going along. At least then he could keep an eye on her. He was suspicious about the long-term effects of the glasses. He refused to wear them, and Alta refused to give them up.

℗

They walked in the direction of the rocks and outcroppings they had originally gone to with Radisson, but he wasn't there.

Alta stood still silently and watched the citizens, calculating their movements, trying to find the pattern. It was as if there were eddies, invisible swirls. She had left her glasses behind so she wouldn't be distracted.

Alta followed the drifts, stopped and watched, followed the drifts again. They walked farther than they ever had, and Billy recorded landmarks as he went. As if, Alta thought, as if it *all* wasn't three rocks and a bit of sand, turn left, four rocks and a bit of sand.

And then, quite suddenly, there was Radisson. It was a night of slightly more light, so it was easy to see him, standing on some rocks, gesticulating. He appeared to be talking to someone, pleading with someone. He had an idiot grin. Citizens drifted around him.

Billy called out to him, as did Alta. They hurried, afraid he would run away, but he paid no attention to them.

"Hi," Billy said. "Everyone's looking for you. We came to bring you back again."

Radisson shook his head. "Not yet. I'm kind of busy right now. With Harriet." He grinned. "I've been telling her how much I've missed her."

He turned back to his ghost.

"Is this the woman you said died a long time ago?" Billy asked. "She's not real, you know."

"No, of course not," Radisson said amiably. "She's utterly fantastic. How could she be real? But it's still wonderful, isn't it, to be given another chance? I thought I'd lost her forever."

"Take off your glasses," Billy said. "Please."

"No, I have terrible eyesight. If I take them off, I can't see her." He held his hand out gently, his fingers curled in entreaty. A citizen seemed to drift into his grasp or close to it. Alta felt a restless almost-jealousy: his face, even behind his glasses, was joyful. His joy was certainly real.

❦

The glasses were spreading throughout the colony. Everyone had someone they hoped to see again, just as Alta wanted to see the figure of herself again. How had she looked? Like she'd been happy in her life or sad? Like she'd been successful or not? That creature was her future, even if it was only in her own mind, and re-ally—why would her mind be interested in that? There must be some kind of reason for it. Radisson had found the woman who preoccupied his thoughts, apparently. He had been given a second chance. Did his own mind do that, or was it the citizens? The explanations—static electricity, charged parts of the brain—all sounded reasonable, but they were guesses; they were not scientific. It all came back to Filper and his reasoning and experiments. And where did Filper's ideas come from?

Alta asked Billy to put on the glasses; to come with her and see what she saw. But Billy frowned; he looked at her intently; he told her not to wear the glasses, not to sneak off by herself, not to buy into an illusion.

"How can you say it's not real if you haven't seen what I've seen?" she asked. "How can you assume that everything has to be the same here as it is on earth? That there can't be different rules, different—oh, I don't know—ways of being? You'll only see what you *have* seen with that way of thinking; you'll never admit seeing anything new."

He sighed. It was a hard thing to be shut out by her; they had always been in agreement before this. But he promised himself over and over that he would stand firm where the glasses were concerned. The glasses had ruined Radisson, were changing her—he was surprised that they had been allowed for as long as they had—but he couldn't help her if he also fell under their spell.

"You always believed in the truth," Billy said wearily. He had been at it for days, now, trying to convince her that the citizens weren't real, and that reality mattered, it really mattered.

"I only know what my senses tell me," she said. "What makes you think my senses aren't 'real'?"

It was the same argument.

"My mind is still clear," she said. "I just don't agree with all these limits you put on things."

"These 'limits' as you call them—well, I'm limited to knowing what's real and what's not. It was always something you cared about too."

"There are only those two things?"

"What do you mean?"

"Maybe there's something else. Maybe it's not reality and it's not insanity Maybe there are more options. Wouldn't that be interesting?"

He rolled his eyes. "Where would these 'more options' come from? Do you think *science* is different on every planet?"

"Maybe it is," she said. "Why not? Just look at what we have here. Every culture has ghosts and now look—ghosts. Doesn't that say something?"

"I'm still not going to wear those glasses," he said firmly. "You're not thinking the way you normally do. I want to think the way I normally do."

"Then you shouldn't have come here," she said.

The next ship brought Radisson's replacement and two new doctors. A man who had preached to the citizens went home, as did Filper and two others. Billy could see that there was a change coming, an official change. The new people never went outside, and the new director, Chaudry, ordered constant physical and psychological checkups for all the station personnel. They began to confiscate Filper's glasses. They talked about restricting visits outside.

Alta was aware of this; she was aware that Billy watched her and followed her everywhere. She kept changing the spot where she hid her own pair of glasses, but it was inevitable that Billy would find them and take them.

On the morning when she realized the glasses were gone, she composed herself and went out to find her citizen.

Billy followed her.

Over a ridge and down an incline, citizens in their groups of three or four wavered for a moment, and then they began to wander towards her.

Alta thought it strange that all of them were moving toward her, not just the one who looked like her. Without the glasses, of course, she couldn't see which one that was.

The first citizens arrived. They held out hands to her, and it was automatic, she held her own hand out, though she knew of course that there was nothing substantial there, nothing to hold on to.

But she felt them!

"Alta? What are you doing?"

She turned to answer Billy and saw that he had a peculiar heaviness to him, as if he were made of a rock or a tree trunk. The hand he held out to her was startling in its strangeness. Alta moved aside to avoid it and glanced at her own arm.

The sleeve of her shirt was white and sheer. She looked down and saw that all of her was white and sheer. A small wind rolled through her chest; it wasn't displeasing; it was oddly light and soothing. It made her sway gently. She asked herself with a bit of detachment, hadn't she ever felt the wind on Nox before? It felt like little fingers tapping for attention, but tapping from the inside. This was an amusing thought that caused her to sway back and forth with the various words of the thought.

For a brief moment, she wanted to explain this to Billy, as she always had with new ideas, but his face was distant and aloof.

He kept reaching his hand out to her as she stepped away. His eyes seemed to look past her; or was there something he was looking at behind her? She wanted to turn and see, but everything was against it. The wind, the way her clothes rippled and spread in the breeze, the strange disinclination of her body to move quickly…it reminded her of something. Yes. Being washed by waves, chest-deep in clear water. One of the great sensations. How the body appreciated it. Resist and release. Movements were intriguing.

"What are you doing?" Billy asked in shaky bits of sound.

She opened her mouth to answer and then paused with it open as she considered which word to begin with. Her eye caught the sight of fellow citizens grouped in a thought, perhaps even in a word. She felt a gentle welcome.

"Alta!" Billy said. "Can you hear me? What's happening to you?" His last question was said with a kind of gulp, a big influx of air in and an explosion of air out.

She leaned toward him because his voice had pulled her a little. There was no reason to abandon this new sensation; not yet. She would just stay here for a moment, and join him later.

The citizens wavered together, and she liked the agitation, it made her shiver in the wind. She had liked amusement rides in her childhood, when they shook her and pushed her around, when she felt unmoored. She moved off and recovered the balance she'd found in drifting with the wind. She swayed over to the citizens gathered near a crest of rocks. Their thought was to do with the rock.

Billy took her hand and pulled her away, and she let him. There was no reason to resist anything. But she was indistinct for a while, when they got back to base. She stood and swayed until gradually the feeling left her.

"I almost understood," she told Billy. She looked out a window and thought, for the first time, how peaceful it all looked. *They* almost understood as well, she thought, but she kept that to herself.

AdAstra Mining recalled all its employees and left Nox alone. The company sent down cameras to rove around the sandy landscapes. Nox looked the same, with three rocks and a rise here, and three rocks and a dip there.

Scientists studied the data and confirmed that there were indeed strong electromagnetic readings. The ghosts certainly were at the end of the visible spectrum. The citizens clustered and released, their open mouths howling soundlessly, their sheeted hands waving warnings or beckoning carelessly. They showed up that way even on long-distance transmissions. There would be no decision on whether they were sentient or not.

AdAstra Mining found another planet that was almost as worthwhile as Nox. It was an easy planet, with only small vertebrate life and huge wind storms. It was a relief to deal with understandable problems. There was no question about getting ghosts to sign a contract.

The president of the company stepped down after the whole Nox fiasco, and the ships that went out that far looked at Nox with curiosity or wonder, and then passed by.

The Moons of Martle Hart

"Did something just come in on the Board stream?" Ensign Carly Lipper asked, twisting slightly to peer over at her companion. She was in a small flyer making the sweep around the gas planet Martle Hart and its three newly occupied moons, regular duty, nothing remarkable. It was a form of border patrol, seeing if any unknown ships were approaching, checking the Boards for calls for help.

"All sorts of things," Lieutenant Janet Bango answered, head bowed, tapping away on the virtual keyboard. She was currently in the second seat, to Lipper's left and slightly behind her, facing the Boards' screen. "I think there's some serious fun going on out there; I can't believe any of this stuff is true," she said in mock exasperation. "Maybe it's a test."

Lipper nodded; she always suspected tests. "Or maybe they're bored. Though they've been given training, so they shouldn't be making things up."

In fact, she wondered if Bango was a kind of test for her. She'd met Bango on Halliburton, the first moon colonized by the private exploration corps. Maybe she should have double-checked the orders. She hadn't paid that much attention; her mind had been on the upcoming flight, her first solo mission, and she'd been disappointed when Bango had come up, introduced herself, and told her they'd be flying together.

Lipper had stiffened to attention slightly. Lt. Bango outranked her, of course. "I was told I was going solo, sir," she said. Her eyes looked straight ahead, but she had already mastered the art of peering sidelong. Lt. Bango was amused.

"They do that. They change things," Bango said cheerfully. "I'm supposed to be on leave. Not that it matters. For me to be able to really be on leave, I'd need six months just to get there. Hey, life's an endless bus trip, isn't it?"

Lipper had been influenced by Bango's casualness. She'd felt terribly new, so she'd gone along with it. But there was something about Bango and her casualness that was beginning to bother her.

Bango continued checking through the Boards, those informal exchanges of outer-colony life. They contained logs of what the colonists, who were largely Halliburton military personnel, saw and thought and did. There was a certain amount of freedom on the Boards, and Lipper wasn't sure where that freedom ended.

"It's true," Bango agreed. "They shouldn't make things up. But who really knows what goes on in people's minds?"

There was a minute of relative silence, as Lipper ran her hand over the operations screen, checking systems. She had the forward seat, watching the flyer's systems and the radar. This also held the command channel, relayed through Halliburton to the nearest battleship, should anything go wrong.

"Did you read it, the Board from Padrasol? Kind of disturbing." Bango said and waved Lipper over to read it.

"This is the day-shift Board," Bango said. "Read it and weep."

I don't think it's a good idea to stay here much longer. They don't have a good effect on us. I feel uneasy about them, though I doubt they'd be violent. No, there's something else going on here. I think they may make us mad, eventually. Already I can feel my mind slipping; it's almost as if I understand something horrible, or almost agree with something horrible. You see—this is part of it, this indistinctness. I am a decisive man, yet I find myself faltering. They know who we are; that's part of it. They come up to us so eagerly. And some of the team are beginning to feel that eagerness, too, and I can't imagine there's any good coming from it. Why would we be so eager—why would they be so eager—we are aliens to each other. It is unnatural.

I begin to suspect I know what the attraction is between us. They never speak, but we have begun naming them, and we agree on the emotions or thoughts we ascribe to them. Astra—a female—is young, and Almira—another female—is older, but still lithe and vibrant. They are both intense, wanting to search us and find an explanation. I don't know if it's an explanation, really; they want to know about us and our pasts; we all agree on that in general. They are curious about us, overwhelmingly curious. Happily, eagerly curious. But they don't speak, and we don't know if they can read minds, each other's and even ours; we don't know what they want or know. But I can swear it's not neutral.

"Have you ever been to Padrasol?" Bango asked.

"I've only been to the academy on Halliburton," Lipper said. "Just got here ten days ago to complete my training, when they assigned me to the patrol. Padrasol is the latest outpost, isn't it? The farthest out?"

"That's right," Bango said. "First one if you're coming from the other direction. That's the other way to think of it. Typical bipedal aliens with the strange hands, just like on Halliburton and Clovis Ack."

"I haven't heard anything about any trouble here. Just complaints about the food. And jokes about the locals, of course."

Bango nodded. "Everyone complains about food," she said. "I was on Padrasol recently. We tried to make the food look like something else so we could eat it. Everyone was getting cranky."

"Ah," Lipper said. "Maybe they're just letting off steam. Anyone else talking about it?"

Bango scrolled backwards. "Looks like it's just this one guy."

"On Padrasol."

"Not a bad moon. There are some crawling mosses there as well. I look forward to seeing them again once this tour is done."

"Oh, right, I think I've heard about the mosses," Lipper said. "Walking plants. I wonder what that means."

"Means? Locomotion is common to animals. I've seen them. You start to wonder whether the plants are moving or the plants are staying put and the moon is moving."

"An interesting way to think of it," Lipper said.

Actually, Bango was interesting. The quarters were horribly tight, but Bango was good at staying out of the way—much better than Lipper was—and she didn't get annoyed at Lipper's clumsiness. She moved smoothly and almost jointlessly, the way she could squeeze past with a single motion.

Also, Bango was a magician—an old-style one, with tricks and illusions.

On their first day together, Bango had opened her palm and held out Lipper's top jacket button. Lipper had frantically lifted her hand to check her jacket, and yes, her button was missing. She hadn't felt a thing. "How did you ever do that?" she gasped.

"It was easy. Oh, and I think this one is yours, too?" And she held out the button from Lipper's shirt, under the jacket.

Lipper had been dumbfounded.

"I do magic tricks," Bango told her. "I'm very good at them. Would you like to see some more?"

She went through a small act, sneaking a hard candy from Lipper's pocket and making it appear inside a control panel slot. "I guess I should watch you carefully from now on," Lipper said. She was amused despite herself. Their routines were invariable, and here was entertainment.

"I was a lonely child," Bango said, shooing away Lipper's appreciation. "I spent a lot of time reading, and I came across a book of tricks. It turns out I have a talent."

"As a pickpocket?" Lipper asked with a grin. "Are you a magician or a criminal?"

"Oh, well, when I'm around people like me, I'm nothing much. I've seen some great tricks. I once saw someone take the bones out of a hand and then put them back again."

"Oh, that's too much, really; there's a limit to what I'll believe."

"That's fine." Bango grinned. "It works much better with people who don't believe."

❦

The next day, it was Lipper's turn to check the Boards, and she found something interesting from Clovis Ack:

This is a country of thieves and liars and maybe even worse.

You've heard of course that they eat the fingers of their enemies? Perhaps it's not so bad, since the fingers grow back and in fact maybe they aren't even fingers. Six of them, around a palm, like a daisy or something. Maybe they're more like lizard tails, but capable of grasping.

And they hug. I thought at first they were looking for money in my pockets, but in fact they have a natural liking for just suddenly hugging people full-force. Without letting go—in fact they can do it for so long, and it's so appealing, that any of them passing by will glom on to the hug, getting a bigger and bigger crowd with a nugget of human at the center. That's how we lost Blair, smothered in the middle and found an hour later. Do they do it on purpose? Gungel was about to go around a crowd of them yesterday, then thought better of it. He radioed back for support, and we pulled the group apart and found Myerson. She was pale and shaken. She said it wasn't as bad as you'd think, but then again, she immediately applied for a leave.

Because you know they do steal things—it wasn't so absurd at first to think a hug was a way of frisking us down. They take things in front of us, behind our backs, sniff them and taste them and leave them wherever they lose interest. They don't care about our complaints. They steal our food though they don't eat it. They've tasted it and find it wrong. I've seen what they eat—a species of caterpillar or worm, something repulsive and fat that moves slowly.

I request an immediate reinforcement of our team until we figure out what their intentions are. I believe they have intentions.

"It doesn't sound so bad—hugging," Bango said dismissively.

"But someone got hurt."

"I've heard of someone who broke his ankle just tripping on a rock." Bango shrugged. "I mean, accidents."

"Okay, I see your point. But this guy thinks something's going on."

"He gets jumpy around the natives. He thinks they have strange rituals. Well, they probably do. That's what makes travel so interesting."

Lipper scrolled through the Boards. "I don't see any other reports. No one else is talking about it. Nothing beyond this one hugging thing." She pursed her lips. "Non-urgent, then. I'll put it in my Watch-level queue. See what happens next." She nodded decisively and filed it away. "Have you been to Clovis Ack?"

Bango shook her head. "But I have heard about those alien hands, and yes, they are disposable."

"Disposable hands."

"I'd like to get sent there. I think that would be a great place for some new tricks."

Lipper laughed. "What kind of tricks?"

"I could switch their hands. It wouldn't hurt them. But I don't know if they'd care. You see, the only way a trick works is if it matters to the mark. I mean, you have to care if someone steals your watch or your wallet or a photo of your loved one in a red hat."

Lipper straightened up. "Is that a reference to something in particular?"

Bango shrugged. "Why? Do you have a photo like that on you?"

Lipper jumped up and checked her inside pocket. "Bango," she said. "That wasn't nice. It helps if I know I have it on me."

"You have it on you. Check your shoes."

Casting a quick, furtive look at Bango, Lipper unlaced her shoes. When she took her right foot out, a photo tumbled as well.

"I'm not even sure that's a trick. You could have done it while I slept," she said, annoyed. She looked up at Bango.

"Done what?"

She looked down again, and the photo was gone. She looked around wildly, then began to search her pockets, and there it was again, in her inside pocket, as if it had been there all along.

"I wish I knew how you did it," she said grudgingly. "But let's establish some boundaries. There are some things of mine that are off-limits. This is one of them. It's too personal. No, wait." She raised her hand. "It's not that it's personal. It's just that it reassures me. I need to know that it's there."

"A totem object," Bango observed. "I won't touch it again."

"Thanks."

Bango shrugged. "You have lots of other things."

"Oh, I'm going to be watching you. It's all sleight-of-hand, isn't it? Distract me, get my attention on something else. I know that's the theory, anyway."

"That's the theory," Bango agreed amiably. "It's just that I'm very good, Lipper. It's very hard for anyone to see what I'm doing."

Later that day, Lipper found another odd report.

I'm mad as hell. Someone has cloned me without my permission. We set up the second camp on Clovis Ack last month, and just last week I saw my first clone, walking toward the ship. Then each day I've seen more and more. I demanded to know who was doing it, but those bastards I work with each claimed that they were the ones being cloned and the whole planet was filled with their clones. So I shot one of them, and the rest of them ran away. If I see any of them again, I swear I'll get them with one shot, but all I see are the clones of myself, and it's just too creepy shooting myself. I mean, what if they split in two and there are twice as many of them? Is that what clones do? They're wearing exactly what I'm wearing. I thought I could fool them, and I changed my gear completely yesterday, but I was totally floored when they had changed their gear too. Isn't there a law against this? Could someone look that up? Maybe if I tell them what the consequences are, maybe they'll just go away. They can go away, right?

Lipper frowned. "He shot someone? It's really unclear whether he shot one of his clones or one of his coworkers. And it doesn't make the least bit of sense. Clones take a certain amount of time, and he's claiming—what, a couple of weeks?" Her words trailed thoughtfully. "I don't think anyone could do that in a couple of weeks."

Bango shook her head. "He didn't understand what was going on, so he shot someone. Or thinks he did. That's not very good training, is it?"

"You're right; he thinks he did it," Lipper agreed. "There's always someone who panics and lashes out." She stopped a moment to wonder whether she was the kind of person who would panic. "He lost his bearings. But I don't know if that's the point here. All the people said they'd been cloned, and apparently they don't see any clone but their own. That's getting a little, well, contradictory. It's some kind of individual mass hallucination. We should forward these to Central Patrol, see what she says."

"I got that." Bango took over at the comm and verified the transmission. "Sent to CP."

"I don't see how all of these problems can be real," Lipper continued after a moment. "We've been colonizing other sectors for close to 50 years, and the percentage of problems is—we covered it in training—about 10. I mean problems with life support or surface conditions."

"Are we sure there aren't other life forms there? Aside from the six-fingered huggers?"

"That's the hair in the soup, isn't it? What if something's there and we don't know about it? What if it's a rock or an insect or a piece of moss with the ability to drive us crazy?"

"Specifically to drive us crazy? I mean, they evolved just for us? As our enemy? This far away from home?"

Lipper admitted defeat. "That would make no sense at all. Maybe it's just Space Weariness in some new form. Or maybe we're missing something. It's odd that yet another colony is now a little weird. Like it's spreading. Space Weariness can spread, I think."

"Let me show you a trick," Bango said. "While we eat lunch. Grab some food pouches, okay?"

Lipper twisted to the food locker to her right and slightly behind and took out two lunches. "Here," she said. "You always want the green lunch."

"What did you pick for yourself?"

"The yellow lunch. It's spicier." She ripped off the top strip. "It's empty!" she said. "It's all sealed and empty!"

"Let me check mine," Bango said, and Lipper leaned over anxiously. After all, if the food packets were empty, they would have to abort their mission. "No, mine is fine. It must just be yours. Are you sure?"

"Oh come on, there's no mistaking an empty pouch." She lifted up her pouch to show Bango, and her eyes saw the bulge of food, and she smelled the whiff of spices. She poked the top edges apart. "It's all here," she said sullenly. "Another trick. Somehow, I don't like this one at all."

"Messing with food. You're right, it's not such a funny trick."

"You can empty things out and fill them again while I'm still holding them." She could feel her outrage rising.

She reviewed, again, exactly how she'd met Lt. Janet Bango. It was past the security gate and inside the docking area, she was sure of it. So Bango could have come from another ship. She'd flashed some orders, named the right names; Lipper was too new to challenge her.

But what if this was some test? What if she was supposed to suspect Bango of something? Or maybe she was supposed to be a good soldier, no matter what the circumstances. Do what she was told. What if all of it was a test, these strange reports from the moons, these strange magic tricks of Bango's?

Worse than that—what if it wasn't a test? What if Bango was an infiltrator of some kind, an invader?

"Look at this one," Bango said the next day. There was another message, from one of the newer colonies in that sector, the far side of Halliburton.

This place is filled with invisibles. We all felt something, but we couldn't figure it out until recently. But we've started rounding them up. We're putting them in boxes. We can't see them, so we just scoop at the air until the boxes start shaking. We've put them in fires, we've run over them. We can hear them screaming but we're just not sure they're dead, 'cause we-can't-see-them! What if they're still alive, laughing at us? Getting out of the containers when we burn them or bust them? This is a horrible situation. We've started laying down explosives.

"Explosives," Lipper repeated. "Are they going to blow up the invisibles? They can't kill life forms; that's against all the rules."

Bango laughed. "I bet there's not even one invisible in those boxes."

Lipper glanced over at her, then glanced away. A trick. Like the empty food pouch, she thought. "Then what's making all the noise in them?"

"Oh, that's easy," Bango said. "Maybe little ventriloquist dolls. Didn't you say you like ventriloquists?"

"Maybe," she said cautiously. "I think they're creepy in an interesting way."

"There you have it."

"So they'll blow up the boxes and use up all of their explosives."

"Probably all their weapons, too, when the invisibles seem threatening."

"And then?"

"Harmony," Bango said with satisfaction "Everyone sits down to the same feast. They live happily ever after, visibles and invisibles as one. And there will be presents, of course. I bet that's what was really inside all the boxes."

While Bango slept on her off-shift in the rear of the flyer, Lipper sent a message to Central Patrol. "I think I have some kind of alien with me," she wrote guardedly.

She calls herself Lt. Janet Bango — can you check whether I was assigned to someone at the last minute? It was supposed to be a solo flight, but she seemed to have everything in order.

She can change things, empty them out or move them, unless she's doing something to my perceptions. I can't tell. And I suspect she can alter sounds. I don't know what she is, or what she wants.

> I request instructions. She reads all the Boards. I
> don't believe we are alone, Sir.

She sent it off. She looked out at all the stars, all the planets. They had been told to prepare for new forms of life; they were told to be stolid and thoughtful and to move slowly if there was no immediate threat. Of course, it was hard to tell what an immediate threat looked like, sometimes. Especially if they were invisible.

She whipped her head around. She thought Bango was behind her. There was nothing.

She began to feel a little silly. Was she being utterly foolish? What did she know about magic tricks? Perhaps what Bango had done with the food pack was easily explainable. She used the time to research it in the entertainment database, which was pretty thorough. She read how some tricks were done, but she had held the food pouch the whole time, never letting it down, never letting Bango substitute it. Most magic tricks were misdirection, she was right about that. The mark looked somewhere else and missed the switch. Well, in general, she thought she would make a pretty good mark. She followed directions. But she was sure she hadn't looked away.

She studied an easy trick. Holding a quarter in your hand, switching it to the other hand, having it appear behind someone's ear. She practiced it while Bango slept.

Bango always slept for five hours, no more, no less. Lipper tried it a few times, but found she couldn't think as well on just five hours.

❦

They did their routine systems checks the next day, studied the Boards, read out some work details from the assignment logs. There was no reply yet from CP.

"I have a trick," Lipper finally said.

Bango grinned. "This should be great. What do you want me to do?"

"Oh, I want you to keep your eye on the quarter," Lipper said, tossing the coin from one hand to the next. Finally she switched it from her top hand to her lower hand and moved her hands apart. "Where do you think it is?" she asked.

"Behind my ear," Bango said, and pulled the quarter out with her own hand. "That was great," she said.

Lipper got still. Of course the coin should still be in her own hand, but it wasn't. Bango had managed, some-how, to change the trick.

"I wonder how you do that," she said slowly.

"I've left clues everywhere," Bango said.

❦

"Aren't you American descent?" Bango asked the next day.

"Yes," Lipper said. She was feeling subdued. She was having trouble sleeping on her own night shift. What *was* Bango? If she was a new and harmless kind of alien, then it would be great for Lipper to be the first to report it. But if she wasn't harmless? She hadn't heard back from the CP yet; she should wait.

"Let's play an American game, then," Bango said. "It's a travel game. I forget what it's called. But you yell out the nationality of any spacecraft you see. There! Aleleutian!"

"I don't see anything."

"Ferodorov! Clovis Ack!"

"Clovis Ack isn't advanced enough for its own spacecraft."

"Maybe the invisibles are. Another Aleleutian! Aren't you going to play?"

"Are *you* American?" Lipper asked.

Bango shrugged. "Maybe I'm what you'd call American Registered Alien. You know, I wasn't born there but I hooked up with one of them."

"Oh. Did you? You mean you got married?"

"No." Bango looked at her with her smile as wide as a trap. "No. I met you."

Lipper looked out at the stars and the moons and the deep thick dark. "What are you, then?"

Bango burst out in laughter. "Oh, Lipper, don't be so worried. Didn't you go into space to find a great adventure? Isn't it time for a great adventure?"

Lipper steadied her pulse as best as she could. "What are you, then?" she repeated.

"I'm your friend for life," Bango said. "You can take that as a given. You and me, we're bound at the wrist at this point. I'm your dearest friend. Wouldn't you like a dearest friend, Carly? Haven't you been going it all alone for way too long?"

Lipper froze, her hand hesitating on the console.

"It's a joke, Lipper! Just a joke! You're way too tense, but I apologize. I shouldn't tease you like that. Where I come from, we're always having fun. I'm sure you'll get used to it." She pulled a paper flower from the air and gave it to Lipper.

❦

Lipper touched Bango's arm and her hand, as she went about her checks on the console. She wanted to see what Bango felt like. She lifted her hand once and removed a piece of imaginary lint from Bango's hair.

"What's that?" Bango said, surprised.

"You had a bit of something in your hair. It was just a smudge, nothing really. I was afraid it was space lice."

Bango seemed to be fascinated. "Never heard of that."

"Not even at the academy?" Lipper leaped on it. "You didn't go to the academy?"

Bango steadied herself. "I think in my year no one mentioned space lice. Is it new? What's it look like? What kind of problem are they?"

"They get in your hair and they live there and reproduce there and they, I think, suck your blood or your scalp juices. Makes you itchy and causes infections. You know, parasites."

Bango looked thoughtful. "I was in a training class once that said parasites could be useful."

"How can they be useful?"

"Sometimes they can supply what the host doesn't have, say a kind of immunity, or an ability to adapt."

"Give me an example."

"Well, there's a fungus on Spindle colony that gives the inhabitants an emotional steadiness. They love it. It works beautifully. And I think they also claim there's a species of microscopic frog that grants invisibility. It protects both of them."

"Never heard of that colony," Lipper said. "And you learned this at the academy?"

Bango, for the first time, seemed annoyed. She was silent for a few minutes, then she said, "You know very well I didn't learn it at the academy."

That was progress, of a sort. It was, Lipper thought, a half-admission.

❦

There was a small beep on the console. "A message," Bango said. "It's from the CP." She was at the main console.

Before Lipper could say or do anything, Bango tapped the screen, and the message opened even without Lipper's password. "Look at that," she said. "It's all about me. It's asking for more information and advising you to land on Halliburton, in the sealed bay. Well, I guess we can do that."

Lipper eyed her uneasily. "They'll find out what you are."

"Will they? What are you worried about, Lipper? I told you we'd always be friends."

"I choose my own friends," Lipper said. "And it's not you."

Bango twisted her head, to left, to right, and up and down, as if she were clearing a crick from her neck. "But you already belong to me, you know." Her voice was gentle. "You got my attention right away. Those bipedals with the disposable hands just aren't as interesting as you are. We adapt, you know. We can learn to look like anything, anything useful. We're not bogged down like you are. I can show that to you, a little. You'll love it, I promise.

"Here's what I do: I arrive, try out the local species, find the best there is. My species likes other species. We do. We find them interesting. We have a long life-span, and we need new interests. It looks like we have a better sense of humor than you have, but some species we've tried have none at all, and that's incredibly boring. It's really in your own interest to be amusing because I can

94

show you things you haven't even imagined. You'll live a better life with me. I'll show you amazing things."

"I don't want that."

"I'll make sure you're happy and healthy, and I'll do my best to treat you well."

"Like a pet?" Lipper was bitter.

Bango was delighted. "That's it! That's why you have pets, isn't it? Because it's so boring without them? Would you deny that to me, then? When you do the same thing yourself?"

"I'm not a dog or a cat."

Bango laughed. "Oh, no, a dog or a cat wouldn't work at all."

Lipper's mouth was dry as she considered her options. She knew she couldn't outwit Bango. All she could do was gather information. "And then?" she asked. "I mean, when I'm no longer so amusing? I notice you're here all alone. That must mean you grow tired of your—pets, I guess. And then what?"

"Oh, nothing dramatic," Bango said. "We're not cruel. When the time comes, I'll put you down somewhere and let you go free. I can't guarantee where and when, you know, it's up to you. If you want some advice, just be fun. Be fun for a long time." Bango winked at her.

The wink was unendurable. Lipper reached for the comm. And Bango watched tolerantly.

The comm was dead. She tried the screen, and it popped up with a vid of Bango pulling rabbits out of the corner of the vid screen.

Lipper got very still. Bango was indeed in charge and could demand anything at all. Lipper might, someday, figure out how to reach her own kind, or how to escape, or how to attack, but right here and right now there was nothing she could do.

"You see the problem," Bango said gently. "You've assessed everything and made your decision. Good." Her voice was encouraging. "You know the best thing to do is be smart and cooperative and try to keep all your thoughts in the back of your brain. Go ahead and believe you'll be free someday. That seems to help a lot. Maybe I'll let you go on some planet with a species like yours. It doesn't happen all the time, but it does happen. I swear." She made an elaborate play of crossing her heart and swearing—"to what again? Oh that's right, I swear to God!"

Lipper's smile was half-hearted, but it was a start. She straightened up a little, and tilted her head and tried to look friendly. They taught you at the academy that you had to be fully committed to your plan of action once you'd decided what it was. And she'd decided. "Can you show me the trick you did with the food packets?" she asked. "I've always liked tricks."

"That one's way beyond your skills," Bango said.

"Then teach it to me slowly. Let me learn all the skills I need. I want to be like you, to read you, to understand you. As well as I can, of course."

"Good girl," Bango said, delighted. "I knew I'd made the right selection."

Lipper did her best to look pleased. "You can show me a lot," she said. "And I'm eager to learn."

Bango winked at her, and Lipper told herself it was just a friendly gesture.

It would take some time, but Lipper would learn what she could. She would be a pet, she would laugh and be obliging, but she believed—she had to believe—that she would learn enough to someday turn around and kill whatever Bango was, and be released. Like a dog turning on its master, like a cat racing out the door.

Respite

Sor India watched carefully as the Marshal of the Indigenes gazed through the glass wall into the ward. He was slightly jowly, with graying hair and a stiff back. He looked a little bored.

"They look peaceful enough," he said.

"You can see how helpless they are," she answered calmly. "They can't do anything for themselves."

"So I've been told." They both looked at the room full of Durosians, those strange squat creatures with the narrow waists.

Some were propped in chairs while their bedding was changed, others lay in their hammocks, all wearing a kind of institutional smock. Their eyes were closed; they were sleeping.

Sor India was showing the Marshal of the Indigenes around the Respite, a huge, sprawling center housing what remained of the Durosians after their devastating illness.

"Normally they would be gathering food or drawing. You know they don't speak, of course? But they were very active, creating structures from their algae ponds and drawing ideograms, hieroglyphs—whatever you want to call them—on their homes and on the ground."

"Some say it was art they were creating." He glanced at her quickly.

Sor India inclined her head. "Art. Yes. A very popular theory."

"Others say they were incapable of art. That they were not evolved enough. That we wanted to believe it. That, in fact, they have limited intelligence. Insect intelligence."

"The creative impulse has often been held as the symptom of intelligence," she pointed out.

He looked at her with interest. "Symptom?"

"I apologize. I meant symbol." What an odd mistake to make, she thought to herself. She was being too careful. Ma Bish was forever saying that too much carefulness led to more mistakes. She should just try to discover the Indigene's motives and quit worrying that she would reveal too much.

"So you believe they were intelligent—like us?" he continued.

"Do they have to be like us to be intelligent?"

He sighed. "I find it interesting that so many of the supplicants—is that what you call yourselves?—prefer to adopt this air of profound neutrality. Philosophical neutrality."

"We are called simply aides. We are not a religious order."

He gritted his teeth. "So you say. I had a relative here, once, a niece; she left. I heard the descriptions—the grand calling, the life of service, the self-abnegation—"

"No; we don't encourage that; there's too much ego in self-abnegation."

He smiled in triumph. "And yet look at your hands."

They both glanced down to where Sor India's hands clasped each other. The last joint of each little finger was missing.

"Self-abnegation, self-mutilation," he said with distaste.

"Is it important to you?" she asked, moving her hands slightly. "This little bit of flesh?"

"Important enough to keep," he said. "And I know all about the early days, the so-called Days of Remorse. I don't see the point; you didn't expect it to change anything, did you?"

"Do you only do things when you expect them to change something?" She caught his irritated shrug. "Sometimes we do things because the symbolism moves us. The Durosians have four fingers; we destroyed the Durosians; we too will have four fingers in order to show our sympathy. I don't regret it. Some aides cut off the entire finger. Perhaps some future generation will merely paint the nail itself; symbolism does tend to wind down with the years." She turned back to the glass and stared through it. "We're not due for an inspection for a few more months. Can I ask why you're here?"

In the glass, she could see the reflection of his faint, smug smile. "You receive a great amount of money, and these are difficult times," he said. "Some people also wonder about the experimental nature of the treatments in your reports. Is this situation—these conditions," he swept an arm toward the ward, "fair to the indigenous population?"

She controlled her annoyance with an effort. "You should be grateful that so many people are willing to dedicate themselves so generously and purely—"

Again, that knowing smile, and a glance at her hand.

She curled her fingers, hiding the amputation. She cocked her head and forced herself to smile. "Without us, they would die. Would that be fair to the indigenous population?"

"Moral fetishism," he said smoothly. "You admire your own beliefs. But a cure would, of course, end this good life you cherish."

"We have a spiritual calling—"

He waved his hand. "Of course you do. Very spiritual—and very comfortable. You maintain them, and we maintain you. In that way, I suppose we're spiritual as well. But for now, I would like to have you show me the rest of the building. Then I'll meet with your financial people. Then research."

"Of course." She inclined her head slightly. "Your visit overlaps with a linguistic symposium. The Durosian culture has inspired a great deal of interest throughout the worlds. Another reason to bear in mind how important their guardianship is."

"The Respite is very good at getting value out of the Durosians," he said. He walked just enough ahead of her—mere inches—to make it seem like he was leading as they passed the wards where the Durosians lay sleeping.

The Durosians were about five feet tall, with a pear-shaped bottom and a narrow waist. Their arms were long in proportion, with four-fingered hands. The fingers ended sharply, a step beyond fingernails, a step before claws. They used these to scratch ideograms in the dirt, in the sides of their cuplike structures; they used them to push seeds into soil, to gather the cloth-like algae on the ponds that surrounded their villages, from which they fashioned everything from plates to simple serape-like coverings against the wind and rain. Their large eyes had golden pupils. Their mouths were wide and thin-lipped; they made no vocalizations.

"You were here before the illness, I believe?" The Indigene stopped and peered at the aliens.

Sor India and the Indigene watched the Durosians do nothing.

"Yes. I liked them. They were strange at first, but they didn't have any animosity. *We* did. Some of the settlers, after a while, began to amuse themselves by tormenting them. Ripping up the algae; destroying their ideograms. Other things." She looked away. "Most people are good enough. Some people are not good enough. There were problems, and not from the Durosians—or at least, how would we know if they were complaining? We lost our best linguist to the illness, before he figured out their markings. So we know very little about their beliefs."

The Indigene just stood there, his head lowered, his hands clasped behind his back. It was an unusual stance, Sor India thought, somehow…old-fashioned.

"What do you think is the meaning of life?" she asked unexpectedly.

He turned slightly and raised his eyes.

"Their life, for instance," she continued.

He turned back to look at them through the glass. His eyes traveled slowly across the rows. "It hadn't occurred to me that their life had meaning," he admitted.

Sor India had emigrated after the Fire in the Plains killed her family and the life she knew. She wanted not to grieve so much, not to care so much, and she chose a life that was alien, and a place that was alien, and hoped to become an alien herself, someone who saw and thought and felt things that had nothing to do with everything she'd lost.

A few months after Sor India arrived, the settlers heard reports of a rogue flu on earth. It spread outward with the supply ships and transports, eventually reaching Duros. It devastated the settlers and—shockingly—struck at the Durosians as well. The aliens were listless for a few days but then became essentially catatonic, struck down in a different way by the same disease. After a week or so, they closed their eyes and slept.

Some of the original settlers created the Respite. They felt responsible—they were responsible—for the devastating illness that had struck the planet. They were soon like a religious order; they had beliefs and a mission and a sense of sacrifice combined with high moral rigidity.

They also felt an enormous sense of fulfillment. Their lives were selflessly devoted to others, and it gave them value and uplift. But Sor India knew a secret; their work was no longer pure.

And so she had asked the Indigene: "What is the meaning of life?"

The tour was over, and the Indigene stood at the window observing the human settlement. "You have how many people here?" he asked, looking at the city that stretched away from the Respite.

She was sure he knew. "A little over two hundred thousand now; new settlers arrive every month."

"It must be getting crowded," he observed. "For the humans. But the Durosians: have there been any more awakenings?"

"Yes," she said carefully.

"And births this year?"

"We've had six new ones before the parents slept again."

"I find it interesting that it's always a mixed group that awakens," he said. "Never all male or all female. Always long enough to have offspring."

"It *is* strange," she agreed. "Maybe nature controls these things. Though we're hopeful that our tests are producing results. That extract we've been working on; we're very hopeful. We think it has helped some of them to waken. But eventually, of course, they all slept again."

"This sounds like the same report as last year." He looked at her sharply.

"It's a consistent development, yes."

"How interesting that it's consistent," he said easily.

She caught him nodding to himself. Had he heard something? Ma Bish always advised her to refrain from leaps of suspicion; her leaps were often mistakes. But her palms were beaded with moisture.

She escorted him back to the main entrance, where he bid her farewell and walked off to the administrative wing. There he could look up records and costs and sneer at whatever he came to sneer at.

Of course, there was a hierarchy at the Respite. The inner circle were recognizable: except for Ma Bish, they had all given up digits for their devotion. The ritual had begun with the first rush of guilt and had developed into a sign of dedication.

Ma Bish had never sacrificed her finger, though she was founder and director. She had never forbidden it, either, maintaining an august neutrality. Only once had she referred to it, a casual comment to an early visitor: "It cuts down on suicides in this population."

Sor India had heard this shocking statement. What suicides? Of course many of the aides had been traumatized; she had. The aides all knew clarity and simplicity now; they had lost their personal lives, and they now had peace—but which came first? Which resulted in the other? Did charity require sacrifice and thus result in good, or did good require sacrifice and thus result in charity?

The front buildings of the Respite were for the tourists. There was the Cultural Center, with its educational offices and its housing for the many conferences the Respite encouraged, and behind it a large plaza, where a Durosian village was preserved, with holographic images of Durosians going about their day. To the right of that and up a small hill, still visible in the distance, was a (now very small) marsh where the algae that the Durosians had used for all aspects of their lives was gathered. The holograms magnified the size of the marsh and showed figures cutting the algae and bringing it back. All visitors were warned that a plant growing along the path was irritating to humans, causing pustules on the face and groin. There was even a photo in the Welcome Center displaying it. Other holographic Durosians gathered nuts and seeds outside the village, children gathered in groups, playing with styluses, adults scratched ideograms on the sides of the cuplike houses or applied new sheets of algae to their dwellings. They made no sounds, and humans expect sounds, so there were recordings from human villages (children laughing, dogs barking). Visitors didn't notice.

Ideograms were everywhere, of course, appearing as translations next to the universal signs by the in-desk, alongside the check-in and baggage trolleys; they appeared on and in the hand-helds, along the collars of the staff, on any and all informational material, and the staff were rarely questioned about it. People expected foreign languages in foreign places. It didn't matter that the pictograms had been chosen randomly.

The actual Respite was behind the Cultural Center and to the left, two fat buildings filled with sleeping Durosians and the humans who cared for them. Sor India left the Respite to look for Ma Bish in the Cultural Center, where a seminar on Creative Markers was in session.

Ma Bish stood outside the graduated auditorium, greeting people. She nodded briefly at Sor India and asked if their visitor was satisfied. Ma Bish was small and self-contained, as if she were made of guarded information. Her voice was rich and low.

"Not at all satisfied. He says he's commissioned to spend days here, unspecified days."

"His temperament?"

"Intelligent but bureaucratic in his thinking. Sees what he intends to see. I'm not sure what that is. Focused very much on money."

Ma Bish clicked her tongue in annoyance. "We'll have to wait and see then."

They paused as a small retinue caught sight of Ma Bish and came rapidly forward.

"I am convinced," the leader of the group said, his hand extended, "even more than usual of the intelligent scrawl theory. Precursors; precursors; nothing more. They liked the way it looked."

"Professor Gibbons," Ma Bish murmured, shaking his hand. She took gentle hold of the professor's elbow, and the group proceeded into the auditorium and up to the dais, where five chairs faced out to the audience behind a table.

"A reasonable theory," Ma Bish agreed. "Though the speaker from the Alien Languages Department is set to prove she sees lingual markers."

"Professor Whellow?" Professor Gibbons asked unhappily. "She sees those markers everywhere. I hear some students tricked her once with chicken scratchings—"

"An old, sad story, sir. She used chicken scratchings once to illustrate the *lack* of precursors. Her enemies delight in twisting it."

The conference was an important step in Ma Bish's plan to make the Respite self-supporting. She used everything she could to raise money, determined to someday be free of the need for grant moneys and government regulations. That day never seemed to get closer, yet Ma Bish never faltered.

The Durosians were clearly a communal society, as witness the arrangement of the cuplike homes around a central plaza. But bees make architecture, it was pointed out. And ants forage and cut pieces of foodstuff and return with it, as the Durosians did with their algae. Sor India resented these remarks, but Ma Bish was noncommittal. It was always better to let them theorize, she said. It kept the Durosians in mind, and that kept them alive.

Ma Bish's steady eye soothed everyone. She looked openly at every aspect of life.

"Do we know how long they live?" she had once asked at a staff meeting.

It was an obvious question, but it unsettled everyone. Ma Bish let the question hang in the air minute after minute, as murmurs rose to a crescendo and then fell back again.

"And how often do they breed?" was Ma Bish's next question.

The voices rose again.

"Do we choose to let them become extinct before we find out how to cure them?" she asked finally. "Or do we find a way to breed them?"

The question shocked and thrilled Sor India. Ma Bish allowed a debate among the newest aides to become heated while she watched serenely, her sharp eyes noting reactions. Finally she said, "Of course we can't breed them like cattle," and the ones who had argued for exactly that clamped their mouths shut. Ma Bish's eyes traveled over the assembly, noting who had said what. She kept track of their position in every discussion she raised. Could they be bred? Would the children be awake or asleep? How would such children be reared? How would this be viewed by the outside world? How indeed would *they* view it?

And thus, with Ma Bish's sharp eyes and sharp ears, certain new recruits became permanent, and certain others discovered they had no talent for it. Sor India often studied the winners and losers and asked herself, Did I see that choice? Very often, she did not.

Sor India left the auditorium to return to the main building, where many Durosians slept and others had been awakened. There were twenty-six awake at present, so she had lied to the Indigene earlier. But the Respite never actually reported the full number ("Why tell them everything?" Ma Bish had asked). The Durosians were destined to fall asleep again, sometime down the line. They knew now that Durosians had one or two offspring after a five-month gestation. The infants began to walk at three months and were often kept in a kind of central nest, cared for by multiple adults.

If the Durosians died out, then the mystery of their scratchings died, as well as any other social behavior that would have become apparent had the influenza not intervened. Maybe they had a dance, a sacred ritual; that would startle the worlds. There didn't seem to be a mating ritual; the Durosians paired off or grouped off in corners. The Respite had tented off the corners when nothing happened the first year; now there were matings and births. They were taped from start to finish, and the tapes were archived.

And then that group went to sleep again.

The Respite had learned how to waken them and cause them to sleep again. The wakening involved a series of synthesized extracts from the algae. Causing them to quiesce meant reintroducing the flu (in any variation) and then keeping them from moving. This apparently triggered a kind of hibernation, which must have had a purpose somewhere in their history. This knowledge had grown gradually over the years; the lower orders of aides understood that the wakenings were a result of the Respite's scientific programs, and the inner circle ruled over how many, for how long, and how often.

Sor India had wavered, once, about inducing them to sleep again. Ma Bish had taken her to the same window the Indigene had looked out, overlooking the human city. "Where do you put the Durosians?" Ma Bish had asked. Even then, years ago, the human settlements had spread out across the landscape. Most of the algae ponds the Durosians used had been reclaimed for fish and drinking reservoirs. One algae pond had been annexed to the Respite, and it formed the pond seen from the mock Durosian village in the courtyard, which had been reconstructed with visitors in mind. Durosians didn't normally live on top of each other; they clustered in groups of two to seven; family groups, they supposed. It was easier for the Respite if all the cups were drawn together into a honeycomb, and as long as the Durosians slept, what difference did it make to them?

Sor India had understood Ma Bish's question, "Where are the Durosians?" immediately. Her eyes traveled from one building to another, awash with human light. She saw the streets laid out in a distinctly human pattern, with vehicles and tram stops and storefronts. There were trees now, slightly stunted and genetically adjusted, but trees nonetheless. It was hard to see any remnant of Durosian life. In every meaningful sense, the Durosians were gone.

They had accepted the first arrivals of humans, they had bent to the effects of the influenza, and now they slept like so many mice in the Respite's many walls.

But not pet mice. When awake, the Durosians clumped together silently, or hid in the mating tents the Respite had provided so auspiciously. Then they went back to sleep and had to be tended to, always. They had to be fed and cleaned. They had to be turned so they wouldn't develop sores. Even the new aides learned the routine within a week. Time had come to be sticky for humans; too many things looked alike from day to day; they became insular, they became suspicious of anyone but them. They loved their Durosian charges and felt free to hate them occasionally too.

The next day, Sor India was passing through the mock Durosian village. She was used to the constant holo display of *A Day in the Life of the Durosians*—she knew every form, every movement as the natives walked up and down the hill. It had been playing, with few pauses, for nearly ten years, so she was quick to notice an unusual form among the Durosians going up to the marsh.

It was the Indigene.

Should she go for Ma Bish, or should she follow him?

If she followed him and needed help, she would have to come back for Ma Bish. They had no radios, because they "honored" the Durosians' lack of technology.

The Indigene, taking long, slow steps, strode up the hill.

She ran through the hallways, looking for Ma Bish, who was talking to a member of the previous day's panel. Ma Bish saw the panic on Sor India's face and excused herself, moving forward to intercept her.

"The Indigene is going up to the pond," she said, panting.

Ma Bish's eyebrows flew up; her eyes flexed open wider. She moved forward to the door, passing another aide, Sor Bim, whom she ordered to find Fro Remy and Fro Catalan, the strongest members of the security team, and send them to the pond.

Up ahead, the holo images continued unopposed as Sor India and Ma Bish streamed through them. Sor India looked back as they neared the top and saw Fro Remy and Fro Catalan at the bottom, hurrying.

They reached the pond, and saw no one.

They went up the well-worn path behind the pond and reached the top of the hill. No outsiders came here because of the toxic plant the Respite talked about so frequently, but in reality, there was no toxic plant. There was a wide, flat field that stretched on for a few hundred yards.

Plastic structures, a little under five feet high, were spread in rows throughout the field. They looked like composters, perhaps, or strange funerary blocks, except for the air slots in the front. Dozens and dozens of them, neatly and exquisitely paced, all facing exactly the same way.

The Indigene was in the third row, pacing slowly. He leaned down a little, where there was an opening, a wide slot. He peered in, then moved on to the next plastic box. He didn't notice them approaching. They saw him put his fingers in the opening and pull, as if trying to open a door. It didn't move.

They approached the Indigene. He heard them, finally, and turned, his face stricken. "What have you done?" he whispered. "What is this, this—horror?"

"This is a step in their cure," Ma Bish said, trying to control her voice. Perhaps the Indigene wouldn't notice the strain that Sor India heard clear as could be.

"Why are they in these boxes?" He put a hand out, steadying himself.

"I said, it's part of the cure," she repeated.

"It is not," he said. "It just couldn't be." He peered into the slit. "In every box there's an animal, just standing there. No sounds. No movements. Just the eyes looking back at you."

"Not animals. Durosians."

"In every box," he repeated. He straightened up, and his eyes roamed over the field. "Locked in. Isolated. Deprived. Do you feed them? Give them water? Or whatever it is they need?"

"Of course," Ma Bish said stiffly.

"Open up the boxes immediately," the Indigene said. "This makes no sense. It's torture, pure and simple."

"You'll just make it harder on them if you open the boxes. We'll have to start all over again."

Sor India could see the tightness of Ma Bish's upper lip, the way her back and her shoulders had fused. She was fierce, fighting for the Durosians. Sor India could only hope to have her clarity someday, her determination and exceptional tenderness, taking on the responsibilities that others would shirk.

"Let them out," the Indigene said angrily and haughtily. "I demand to know why you've done this, how many you've done this to. How long has this been going on? I've never seen anything like it." His face was pale; his voice was harsh. "You've been hiding them," he said. "You've kept them away from anyone who might object."

Sor India could see how he was trying to control himself. She fought back an impulse to insult him and his ignorance; how could he presume to tell them how to serve the Durosians—this man who came only so he could find out a reason to take away the grants? She looked again at Ma Bish's face; she knew the Director would decide, quickly and fairly, how to deal with the Indigene.

"Fro Catalan," she said quietly, and the Indigene's eyes flicked to the aides, who came and stood by Ma Bish. There was a firmness in her voice—though Ma Bish was never soft, this was a decisive, regretful voice. Sor India felt a momentary quaver in her chest.

The Indigene was watching carefully now; his eyes sweeping around to left and right and then coming back to settle on Ma Bish's face. "I'm sure there's an explanation," he said finally. He felt, too, that a decision had been made, and it was not a good one for him. His anger had morphed into caution. But it was too late for caution; Sor India could see that.

"Fro Remy, see the Marshal of the Indigenes to his room, would you, please?" She smiled strangely, her head slightly tilted, looking just to the right of the Indigene's head. "And make sure he's got everything he needs. But keep him in his room."

Fro Catalan and Fro Remy each took hold of an arm. The Indigene twisted and turned, trying to break their grip, but they were larger and well trained. They dragged him down the hill, protesting. His voice rose in pitch, melting into the background noise they had provided for the Durosian village. It was hard to respect him, but Sor India struggled with his fate.

"What will you do?" she asked, her eyes averted. She pulled herself up. Of course Ma Bish would make the right decision.

"We could put him in the boxes, with the Durosians," Ma Bish said. She had begun to walk the line of the boxes, stopping at each to peer into the small rectangle. Out of each rectangle a pair of eyes watched back. Food and water would come for them regularly until one day the caretakers would look in through the slots and find the Durosians' eyes closed, their bodies leaning against the walls of their compartments, asleep again.

"You won't kill him?" Sor India asked. She had almost not had enough nerve to ask. It would show a lack of faith, or a lack of commitment.

Ma Bish looked at her with disappointment. "We are a *charity*," she said.

Sor India looked out into the field, at the boxes. She struggled with it all, but the word *charity* cut sharply through her doubts. These were her people at the Respite; she would always stand with them.

Two days later, Ma Bish sent a report to the Council on the Indigenes, relaying the information that the Marshal had defied all instructions and gone into the labs, where research included working with the live virus. Indeed, she said, he seemed a suspicious man. He had obviously touched or breathed in something he shouldn't have and was in a coma. The Respite was prepared to care for him for as long as necessary and would merely ask that the next person sent should be cautioned to follow procedure.

"Will they believe this?" Sor India asked.

"What part of it is untrue?" Ma Bish countered. "We are a registered research facility; we have the live virus. Everyone knows that. Such things happen, and I suspect he was known for sticking his nose in where he shouldn't."

"Yes. Of course."

There was an uneasy silence, which Ma Bish broke. "He would have changed all of it," she said finally. "You know that." Her eyes lingered on Sor India, who could feel the sympathetic firmness.

"I do. I know that." There were no other options. The Indigene might have challenged the grants, and what then? They couldn't revive the Durosians just to release them into a changed planet. They all knew the Durosians were too gentle to survive for long.

Their decision had been to keep them alive at a cost, and though the cost was drastic, it still seemed the right thing to do, even if what they had ended up with was a kind of breeding zoo.

It was a suitable irony that they had to put the Indigene into a medical coma in order to protect the Durosians.

"A difficult man, looking for a way to destroy all we've done, all the sacrifices we've made. Surely there is some justice that he has joined the Durosians in their sad fate. Surely it is proper that at least one human being suffer with them for what we have caused. Maybe there should be more." She placed her hand gently on Sor India's forearm. "Do you think there should be more?"

Sor India felt herself flush. She was grateful to be consulted. "There can't be more," she said. "Without arousing suspicion or getting a specialist team here for investigation. This is delicate."

"We are the only beings in the universe who care what happens to the Durosians. That may sometimes seem bitter to you—that we care for them, but the only way we can save them is to let them sleep. After all, what have we saved them for if all they can do now is dream?" She lowered her voice. "*If* they dream."

"Of course they dream," Sor India said quickly. "But with the Indigene," she hesitated. "With the Indigene I wonder if we've passed a certain point. If this is no longer charity but a kind of new enslavement."

She looked hopefully at Ma Bish. Her heart beat in her wrists; the thought of antagonizing Ma Bish was so outrageous that it almost made her doubt her own sanity. She appealed to Ma Bish wordlessly to forgive her.

"Do you love me?" Ma Bish asked suddenly.

Sor India's heart lost its balance.

"Do you love these poor Durosians? I have always seen something special in you—kindness; caring; the ability to carry burdens without comment. But I've never asked you directly. Do you love us only within limits or do you love further than that? Do you love to the point where you might do something others consider wrong, or are you unwilling to give up your righteousness? Are you willing to sacrifice your own pride to save them? To save all of us against the world the Indigene wants to enforce?"

Sor India had to close her eyes for a moment, to get her mind clear. She had given years of service without asking herself what she got in return. Her service was her life. There was no other life.

She opened her eyes. Ma Bish looked at her with love within her eyes. Sor India felt taller, stronger. She would earn that love, she would spread that love, no matter what task she bore. This would be her duty: to protect and serve the Durosians, to love and serve the Respite. She felt a flood of peace and certainty. Ma Bish smiled and said, "I know we'll succeed now. We gather together and protect each other. We gather together and love each other." Her eyes were looking particularly sharp—was it tears that brightened her eyes?

Sor India knew that this was what charity was; this was what it meant to belong to charity, and to give charity, and to see charity spill from Ma Bish's eyes, almost touching her.

She rejoiced.

Which Side Is the Other Side?

A hand emerged, wiggled around in the air, then the full arm came through. Finally a head popped out, looked cautiously around, and the whole body followed.

Melba was inside her house, looking through her window to the hedges when it happened. She was in a bad mood. Third person this month, coming through the portal.

Melba was pretty sure she knew who had put the portal there. She had a long-standing dispute with her neighbor, Baldruth Jenkins, about a water line. She was pretty sure Baldruth had installed that portal just to drive her crazy.

Technically, she had a right to shoot at anyone who entered her property from a portal. She had been too surprised to shoot the first one, had thought about it carefully in between the first one and the second one, and had killed the second one. That was legal, but it made her uncomfortable, so she didn't want to kill any others directly. Plus, she'd had to file a report about the dead body, and reports were annoying.

She went out quickly, smiling and waving gaily, and then punched the interloper hard in the guts. She had a strong arm. The creature fled backwards.

Portals were, of course, illegal because technically anything that went from one world to another was contaminated. And it invited unsavory persons in. They'd had occasions, historically, with people stealing gold and geese and even amassing armies and trying to change the political structure in this country. Some of the strangers said it was an adventure, and all the rules changed when you were on an adventure, but for the inhabitants it was, quite simply, unlawful entry.

How had Baldruth managed it? He was obviously much better connected than she was.

She ran yellow tape around the portal and put up signs with images denoting private property and no trespassing. Still they came.

She set out a lawn chair right in front of the portal and was drinking a cup of tea when (how predictable) a hand snaked through the air.

She had a spritzer next to her chair, water mixed with a foul-smelling plant extract. She spritzed the hand. The odor hung in the air even as the hand retreated hastily.

That seemed to work. It was a week before a hand came through again, this time gloved. She whacked it with a golf club. It retreated.

A day later, she was just coming out of her house when she glanced over and saw a helmeted head poke through, look left and right, and then a person stepped out of the portal. It stood still, its eye on her uncertainly. "Hello, there," it said. "Can you tell me where I am?"

It was time to try a different tack. "You're in a poor but religious place," she said finally and pleasantly. "We share all our meager worldly goods, we don't play sports, we are not merely vegetarian but vegan, and alcohol and cigarettes are forbidden." She smiled. "Plus, no sex. Hence, we're all over 70." She smiled again.

His eyes shifted unhappily. "I don't think so. You're hiding treasure. I'm sure of it."

She frowned. She glanced up to the right. She glanced down to the ground. "Okay," she said finally. "Then I'm the guardian of the door, and you have to answer my riddle. What walks on all fours in the morning, on two legs in the afternoon, and on three legs at night?"

He laughed. "We had that in high school," he said. "Man."

"Wrong," she said. "Woman."

They glared at each other.

Finally, she relaxed. 'Fine," she said, "I can see I can't win with you. I'll tell you where the treasure is on one condition. You must not be seen by the king who lives next door." She nearly gagged, calling Baldruth *king*. "Instead, you must search for the golden cup under the, under the—" she thought as fast as she could, "—under the statue of Min in the front yard."

"Min?" he asked. "You mean Minerva? I've heard of her."

She shrugged. "We're on a nicknames basis, Min and I. But yes, Minerva." Dealing with these people who came through the portals was hardly worth the effort. They told you what you needed to know; they were easy to read and easy to please. She squinted up at the sun. "You have three hours. If you find the cup, you can leave this kingdom. If you don't find the cup, you'll be shot at sunset by anyone who sees you." The stranger raised his eyebrows in concern. "Be off! Go that way! Through the hedges, and I wish you well, stranger! I wish you well!"

That one never came back. She assumed he hadn't been able to find the golden cup under Baldruth's favorite statue of his ancestor Min. With any luck the stranger would have dug under the statue and toppled it before he was shot. That would be nice.

She sent the next one who came through the portal out on a quest to release all the Stolen Horses with Diamond Bridles, which happened to be imprisoned in Baldruth's stable. The next had to break the Magic Mirror of Summoning in Baldruth's ballroom under dark of night and still of the moon. She didn't see those two again.

Of course, they might have run back and gone through the portal while she was sleeping; they might still be alive. She was a bit skeptical about that.

She did finally report the portal to the authorities, who fined her an excessive amount of money and filed some paperwork. She said Baldruth had put it there, and that meant a very hefty fine against Baldruth if anyone could prove it. In the nature of things, however, it was hard to prove who had installed a portal; all that anyone knew was that she owned a portal.

On the other hand, they would put cameras outside her house and Baldruth's house. With any luck, they would catch him killing one of the strangers, and while killing strangers only earned a small fine, those fines could add up. Plus, if she did it right, the strangers would harass Baldruth past endurance.

She needed to move things along, however. She spent the next day shopping at thrift stores and party favor stores and set up a stand outside the portal, where she waited until a stranger stuck a hand, an arm, a head, and then a body through.

"Congratulation!" she said. "We've been waiting for you. We are a small country in desperate need of a new monarch to wage war against a neighboring king—he's not too dangerous, you know, but they do need to be quashed every so often. You're it, I'm afraid. Would you like to be king? There are a few arduous deeds you'll have to do, though if the legends are correct you'll find them very easy indeed."

The stranger puffed up. "I certainly would like to be a monarch. I come from a very good family that has far too many children so there's nothing, really, for me to do. My oldest brother and sister are co-chairs of the family business, my middle brother is a lawyer, my cousins are financiers and doctors, and they haven't left me much room to excel. I would love to tell them I'm king of something just to show them how wrong they've always been about me. What do I have to do?"

She squinted. "The damsel next door is being held by her father the ogre-and-king against her will. She wishes to immigrate. She is spirited, talented, rich, and eager to please." She eyed her visitor carefully. "A damsel or a gentlemen, however you're inclined," she said. "I didn't look closely. But very agreeable. And if you win the heir or heiress, you inherit the kingdom, naturally."

"But how will that work if she wants to immigrate?" the stranger asked.

She winced. "My apologies. I was bad in school. I meant to say, she wants *an immigrant*. Someone different. She has standards. No one here is very smart." She rolled her eyes. Oh, these strangers. Oh, the things she had to say in order to get them to do what they obviously wanted to do, came to do, would die to do. *Go forth and test yourself,* she should just say. *Go to my neighbor Baldruth and test yourself on him.*

"Over the hedge," she said after a lengthy sigh. "Go over the hedge and through the hedge and across the lawn and up the path, and you'll come to a very big house. Our version of a castle. No moat. But there's an ogre king inside named Baldruth, and you should consider outwitting him or outright killing him. And grabbing his son or daughter, I don't quite remember, and taking charge. It's never wrong to take charge, especially when you're unknown here but come from an important family back home. Everyone likes someone like that."

"I'm assuming there's some, well, some recognizable wealth?"

She jerked herself upright and smiled toothily. "Gold coin. Silver urns. Stock certificates."

"And some risk?" he asked efficiently.

"Bad temper. Trick courtyard. Laws that hate strangers. Popular sentiment will *not* be on your side."

He nodded. "That's only fair. Now, listen, I know there's always a magic item I need. A spell or something? I need a special word or a secret helper or an animal disguise?" His face flushed pink. He seemed very young.

I hate it when they trust me so much, she thought. "The secret word is *lynx*. Use it when you hear a door slam above you. That door is important. There's a genie in the doorknob and you get just one quick wish. You'll wish for a window that opens onto your world. You'll grab the sack of gold by the door and take the girl or the boy, whatever it is, and jump out the window. The ogre will follow you out the window into your world, but he won't fit in your world, so that will be the end of him, he'll pop backwards and he'll suffer a heart attack from shame. Then you and your love, whatever it is, are free to come back through the portal and claim your royal kingdom."

"Sounds simple when you say it," he said happily. "And I appreciate how clear it is."

"Good luck to you!" she cried and slapped him on the back. "Go through the hedge and past the hedge and around the back and along the lawn, etc."

In fact, Baldruth had a young wife (not a daughter or son) who had a temper, and this might even be fun for her. Who knew how she would react to it? But it was bound to be an irritation to Baldruth who, as far as she was concerned, was not an attractive man and always got more than he deserved. The idea of someone prowling around his house and sniffing at his goods and winking at his wife pleased her. She thought Baldruth would, eventually, sort out the situation, but it would disturb him no end, and that was fine.

In fact, the stranger grabbed the girl and the gold and killed Baldruth and leapt out a window not necessarily into his world, but back onto the lawn and over the hedge and through the portal. She saw him exit with a young woman or man whooping along with him. If a portal could slam, it slammed indeed. Maybe he considered everything, and broke the portal from the other side. It's much easier to destroy one from the other side.

She took a walk through her hedges and over his lawn and went into Baldruth's house and saw that it was empty. There were signs of a struggle, and she liked that very much. There was a busted window. There was a door with a knob missing.

She fed all of Baldruth's animals and then she went home and cut down the hedges. And where the portal used to be, she planted a tree.

A very big tree.

The Alien Came Over the Hill

The alien came over the hill
    elongated, with a gravity belt, leaving behind all
    thoughts of home, armed to the teeth, scared and
    young. All superior officers dead; not sure of her
    mission; wishing for home.

The alien came over the hill
    straight into someone else's war. They didn't know
    whose side she was on, so they missiled her. She
    didn't care about sides. She sent the missile back.

The alien came over the hill
    spacegun shooting silently, ducking behind trees,
    two of its arms waving alien gestures, brought low
    by a man screaming, noise being a weapon she'd
    never heard before.

The alien came over the hill
    invisible save for her eyes, which didn't look like
    human eyes and so could creep among the bushes
    and through the hedges, noting everything like a
    burglar.

The alien came over the hill
  looking sharply left and right, holding her empty
  hands up, having done her research. Still, the
  chances were good she'd be killed, so she had a dog
  with her, or really a dog-like thing, which could turn
  bombs into kittens.

The alien came over the hill
  playing pop music out of a speaker on her shoulder,
  twitching her hand like the pope, nodding like the
  queen, bowing before a barking dog seconds before
  she was shot.

The alien came over the hill
  shining; dragging images of more aliens behind her,
  floating like kites. Magnificent, golden, eyes like ray
  guns (they were ray guns), the kind that legends are
  built on, but limping.

The alien came over the hill
  PhotoShopped, 3-D printed, looking like a human
  but with too firm a handshake, found out, rough-
  handled, she pushed a button and sprang up three
  feet away, looking like a woman landing a good
  punch.

The alien came over the hill
  holding out a new energy source, without wires or
  gears, just a thing like a mushroom cap and an aura
  of force. She came in peace. It would revolutionize
  the poor and save this world if only the world would
  agree to be saved.

The alien came over the hill
> like a bullet in its small craft, burning the ground,
> crunching trees. The pilot adjusted her range and
> sped close to the ground, raising a dust devil that
> whirled silently even after she was gone.

The alien came over the hill
> with many things for trade: strange fruits, new
> alcohol, fabrics that fit automatically, shoes that
> changed colors, guns that killed their targets then
> animated them again, shiny trinkets that unmasked
> the truth.

The alien came over the hill
> with short arms and two long tentacles in addition
> to legs that never straightened out, used to screams,
> flight, shots and bullhorns, striding into a suburb
> where all the cars revved up and came at her, riding
> and driving until she was flat.

The alien came over the hill
> She was flat and slow, unpeeling more selves like a
> pack of cards, standing them all in a row as if to say,
> Shoot me, or maybe, Look at what I am.

The alien came over the hill
> and found nothing lovable. Metal things, flesh things
> were there, but nothing of spirit, nothing of mind.
> She went back over the hill and sent her report: no
> more or not yet.

The alien came over the hill
> slowly and stopped often, taking seeds from a pouch, and planting them. A hunter passing by saw the strange creature and killed her, but did not see what she had planted.

The alien came over the hill
> it took days, the alien was small and had feeble legs and wings that didn't work in this gravity. Her food packs were gone and what around her was safe to eat, and what was lethal?

The alien came over the hill
> carrying a gift wrapped in a bow that kept changing color. She left the gift on the side of the ridge and went back over the hill.

The alien came over the hill
> guns blazing, making eerie sounds, her head revolving, leaking a lethal green gas that smelled of alien almonds.

The alien came over the hill
> dressed as a cat, stretching as she walked, eyes recording, turning as a boy shot the cat with the second gun his father gave him.

The alien came over the hill
> just before she died and wrote a message in the dirt, or a map, or her name, before she turned over on her back and died with her eyes open.

The Brief Return of Marianna Napoli

She came back.

No one had ever returned before. There was always a burst of excitement on the approach to the distant planet Everest. How beautiful, how strange, they transmitted, until their ships broke through the atmosphere. And then silence. No final squawks of terror, nothing.

After three missions, the government agency cancelled the program. Even the drones they sent went silent once they entered the atmosphere. It was a large investment, and it was a deep disappointment to have missions go and not return, never to know what happened. Everest became an illustration of government ineptitude.

A joke at first, but then it became a public intoxication. What was there?

Was it so wonderful that everyone who went forgot their duty to relay information, forgot their families and their friends and their governments and their world?

Imagine forgetting your world.

Two billionaires went public with an offer to hire anyone from the government project to come work on their private spaceships. They assembled teams quickly and raced each other to launch day, when they would send an unmanned test rocket. If successful, they promised to send people next.

One rocket exploded on launch. The other one went all the way to Everest, chirping its info happily along the way. The billionaire's website displayed a transmission of the planet as the rocket neared it, and orbited it, and entered its atmosphere. There were countdowns on social media sites, there were lotteries about who would have the closest prediction as to what was waiting there.

From far away the planet was green and blue and granite white, and there were clouds and massive crenellated peaks and large shadows on wide sands. Pictures were sent back to earth, and servers froze up with the sudden impact of all that traffic.

And then the rocket went blind. There was nothing.

But it had looked beautiful from a distance. The ones who predicted that it was desolate and deadly were resentful, but the ones who said it was a paradise didn't exactly convince anyone, either. There was soon an outcry that the final transmissions might be a lie, a piece of propaganda—in fact, some kind of recording. No one could trust anything assembled out of pixels. Pictures had been doctored before.

No one would really know until someone went there and came back.

Then began the years of private spaceships going to Everest, loaded with food and water and protective gear and a return pod to get home. If you volunteered, you were paid a small sum (some said blood money) into a bank account. If you returned, the sum was extraordinary.

Over 40 people went on individual trips to Everest; none returned. The line of volunteers got smaller and smaller. The ones who signed up were often withdrawn after psychological testing.

And then, suddenly, Volunteer 39—Marianna Napoli, 53, of Pinehurst, NJ—came back.

She returned not in her own capsule, but in the capsule of Volunteer 41. That was, she said, so no one would think she'd been hiding out somewhere else, just biding her time. "I don't bide time," she said lightly. "But I know some people do. I understand about suspicions. I'm returning in Jerold's capsule to prove I was really there."

She said this at the televised interview. She smiled a lot. She laughed appropriately. She spoke intelligently and coherently. The doctors had said she was fine. The world was ready to listen to her story. She squinted into the lights and looked down and looked back up. Her hands were clasped together, and she sat on the edge of her chair. Her hair had been newly cut; she wore flattering clothing.

"What is it like?" Wendy Clay, the interviewer, asked, leaning in. She was young and already had a reputation for incisiveness.

"Oh, well, you know I can't really tell you about that. It's an experience. It's ineffable. It's the most incredible place. It's all thoughts and feelings. But I know that's not a good description. There are no good descriptions." Marianna Napoli sighed and smiled. She looked eagerly at Wendy Clay, waiting for the next question.

"What's it look like? Can you paint us a picture?"

"It looks like heaven. Everything is perfect. The temperature is always perfect. The food is great. There's music. Wonderful music."

She smiled and looked expectantly at Wendy, who pressed forward. "Are there people there?"

"Why, yes, all the others who went are there. They're all very happy."

"I mean, are there native inhabitants, people besides ourselves." The interviewer was obviously trying to make her questions simpler.

"Oh. Yes. I think so."

Wendy let that one linger. "You think so," she repeated softly. "You're not certain?"

"You can't possibly understand. Existence is so different. It's so hard to be specific." Marianna looked eager, her lips slightly parted, her body leaning forward.

"Do you still have a body when you're there?" Wendy asked the question gently, as if it were a normal question, though her hand gripped her notepad tightly.

Marianna wrinkled her brow. "Oh. Well, yes, I do think so. Although, I think, it was a much younger body."

Wendy consulted her notes, looking for her next question. She looked at her subject for a moment, frowned, then asked, "Did you eat anything?"

"Oh. How odd." Marianne sounded surprised. "I believe I did, once. It was something very light and delicious. Like a custard or ice cream. Or perhaps a soufflé. An indescribable color, though. Past blue. Past purple. But almost clear." She laughed. "I must sound very silly. But you see, we don't have the words. There are more words there." She nodded.

The interview continued in much the same way. Everything was wonderful, there might have been some buildings, she couldn't recall sleeping but she never felt tired. Everyone was happy and friendly.

Finally, the interviewer asked, "Why did you come back?"

Marianna brightened. She sat up straighter. "Yes," she said breathlessly. "Why would I come back? They wanted me to come back," she said. "I was happy to do it. But now that I'm here, I have to admit, I can't see it. I can't see it at all. Why did they want me to come back?" She leaned forward, eagerly.

"Who are *they*?" Wendy asked. "Were you supposed to tell us something? Or give us something?"

Marianna Napoli's face wavered. You could see the race of emotions: willingness, uncertainty, mourning. Mourning? What was there to mourn? She was home.

"It's time to go back," Marianna said. "Past time." She nodded at the interviewer, removed her microphone, stood up, straightened her skirt, and left.

It was the first time the interviewer had lost a guest, but she took it in stride. "Whatever it is out there, my friends—whatever it is, it must be fantastic," she said to the camera, and smiled sadly.

Of course it was fantastic. It was what anyone wanted it to be, because there was nothing confirmed, nothing concrete, just vague murmurings from a vague Marianna. For some, that meant that Everest had sinister effects; for others, it might be earth that was sinister, limited, or merely misinformed. There was a certain romance about Everest.

For the next few weeks, Marianna appeared on TV, on radio, was interviewed for the paper, for blogs; she wandered off from each of them, saying it was time for her to leave. The billionaire appeared with her a few times and said he was getting a ship ready to take her back to Everest. And, he said, he was auctioning off seats for the next three ships to go there, with the intention of setting up a steady stream of what would be passenger liners eventually.

Marianna smiled dutifully when he described this. She didn't seem to care. She often stared over people's shoulders or over their heads, patient, enduring.

Her ship left a month later. In all, she had returned to earth for six short weeks. Why had she returned? A substantial part of the population thought she had returned to show that Everest was a paradise, to prove that nothing terrible happened there. Another part said it was clearly some kind of enslavement, entrancement. Marianna was no longer functioning normally, and anyone who followed her went into an unknown that sapped away the very things we valued: liberty, self-reliance, self-determination.

Ah yes, but she had said it was paradise, and she returned to it. No one forced her; no once dragged her away.

People could see that Marianna was alive; they could see that whatever strange thing was out there was within human endurance.

The billionaire's transport was full for the next few years. Ships left and never returned. Everyone promised to send some word back, some description, some reassurance.

But no one did, of course. And after a decade or two, the type of person who went there changed. It was no longer the aggressive, outgoing ones, the boastful ones. Eventually the quiet ones left, and then the ridership fell off, and the billionaire, now aging, had to get up an advertising campaign for his ships to Everest, because it was a new generation, and it had been forgotten. The young thought it was just some crazy notion that their parents' generation had had; some kind of silly rumor. "Flying to Everest" became a phrase the young people used, to signal an aging population's gullibility.

The billionaire received a terrible diagnosis from his doctor and eventually took the last flight to Everest. There was a documentary about the whole thing, and once there was a ceremony with all the names of the departed.

And then it was forgotten.

About the Author

Karen Heuler's stories have appeared in over 90 literary and speculative magazines and anthologies, from *Alaska Quarterly Review* to *Clarkesworld* to *Weird Tales*, as well as in a number of Best Of anthologies. She has published four novels and two story collections with university and small presses, and her last collection was chosen for *Publishers Weekly*'s Best Books of 2013 list. She has received an O. Henry award, been shortlisted for a Pushcart prize, for the Iowa short fiction award, the Bellwether award, and the Shirley Jackson award for short fiction.

She lives in New York City, with forays into a hidden forest in New Jersey, having stumbled upon the portal between them many years ago.